My Par

Mark Hurst

My Partner's Friend

Trust in a friendship and a relationship is essential

Wooded Hill Books Limited

www.woodedhillbooks.com

Dedication

I dedicate this book to all our friends and their partners that we have taken holidays with over the years; and should you recognise yourself in this story, please keep it to yourself.

Prologue

The young police officer opens the bedroom door slowly and enters the room, announcing his presence, unsure of what he will find. The wooden window shutters are closed, with curtains partly drawn across them, and his eyes have yet to transition from bright sunlight to the room's low light. But still, he can see them; they are both lying on the bed, not moving, even with the presence of the officers entering the room. The officer and his female colleague rush over to them, eagerly checking both for a pulse, looking for a glimmer of life to work with. But there is nothing, no breath, no pulse, no life; both are dead and have been for some time.

1

Melissa – The Wild Boar Inn, Bramblehurst

Saturday 10th June

As we enter the Inn, the first thing that hits me is the pleasant setting. It is cosy with a dominant fireplace, low timber beams, walls adorned with framed black-and-white photos of the village over the years, old artefacts hanging from the walls, and the odd hand-painted quotation dotted between them.

Craig heads straight to the bar while Martin, Tanya, and I temporarily reside at a vacant table tucked away in the alcove to the left of the large stone fireplace.

As we remove our coats, Tanya comments, 'This looks nice. I bet they do a great Sunday roast lunch in here.'

Martin replies, 'Yep, I bet they do; I'll go help Craig with the drinks and ask.' I watch him as he crosses the room, saying hello to a couple at a nearby table. This gives me a minute or so to have a quiet word with Tanya.

'How is it all going with Martin; are you two OK now?'

'Yeah, thanks. We're in a good place now. He's got past his writer's block thing, and he's in daily contact now with his editor and publishing company; everything is back on track. It was really scary at one point though.'

'I know. I'm now happy for you both. I presume he's off the meds now and OK to drink?'

'Oh yeh, all good now; I think he intends to party this weekend to make up for lost time.'

'Well then, he's back to his old self,' we smile at each other. I turn my head to look at the men at the bar and continue, 'It's not like Craig needs a buddy to party; he's ready to let off some steam this weekend, with that big case he's working on and the long days into the night preparing.'

'Is he still on that case? It's been going on for some time now. He must be pulling in some big earnings, though.'

I look back to Tanya, 'Yes, I suppose so, but I don't get to see a lot of him these days, not since he joined this law firm.'

'Of course, that's something else we must celebrate this weekend; it completely slipped my mind.'

'Don't worry, he's been playing it down; I think he's a little self-conscious that he is the youngest partner by far in his law firm, although I suppose he should feel proud of his achievements.'

'Absolutely he should; it's well deserved. He wouldn't have done it without you behind him, though.'

'Oh, I don't know. He would have done it with or without me. Once he has his mind fixed on something, he is like an arrow in flight heading to a target. He is driven inside by his passion to prove his father wrong, even though he passed away a couple of years ago.'

'I never did like Barney; he always seemed a bit of a chancer to me, a deal here, a deal there, you know, a bit … shifty, I suppose.'

'Yeh, that was Barney all over, and Craig hated it in him. He loved him as a father, but Craig couldn't respect how his father earned his money. Equally, Barney wouldn't respect Craig's dream of becoming a lawyer and Barney's sailing close to the legal line often frustrated Craig. Respect is a big thing for Craig.'

I register Martin, heading back towards us with two wine glasses and a bottle of wine in his other hand. 'Here we go, ladies, first of many this weekend.' He places the two glasses on the table and starts to pour the rosé wine into each. 'The best the establishment can provide for the two best ladies in the room.'

'Oh, I see. It's going to be one of those weekends, is it? We're starting with the charm offensive already, are we?'

'No, just saying what everyone in here is thinking,' and he winks to Tanya, turns and heads back to Craig at the bar.

I raise my glass and look at Tanya, 'Here's to the return to normality and a memorable weekend ahead. Cheers.'

'Cheers,' she replies, as our glasses clink together.

2

Martin – The Wild Boar Inn, Bramblehurst

Hearing the toast and clink of glasses behind me, it sounds like the ladies are entering into the spirit of the weekend. We've not had one of these get-together weekends in a long time; it must be over a year now since our last trip away. I know I was probably to blame for that, not wanting to do anything, go anywhere or meet people, remaining on my own, at home, retreating to my safe place. Depression got a grip on me; I see that now, and if it weren't for Tanya, I would probably have done something stupid back then. I just got into a dark place and couldn't seem to find my way out.

I was successful at writing; no, I am successful at writing; I must maintain that positive attitude. Winning awards and plaudits is fantastic, and I became accustomed to almost certainty that I would receive them, but when my sixth book bombed, and it bombed badly, I just spiralled; I vainly thought I could write anything and it would be accepted and praised. It was difficult for me to acknowledge and accept the criticism. I know there will always be those out there who use the internet and the review facility to rate poorly, provide brutal comments that don't respect the hard work that has gone into writing a book, the keyboard warriors who seem not to have a good word for anyone but themselves, and I can accept those people will always be there, that's life. Still, when the comments started coming from professional reviews and critics in published media, I took it really badly; this was my career, after all. How dare they? Instead of getting angry and then channelling that energy into accepting and learning from it, I took the other path and hid away.

Through it all, it was Tanya who stayed by me. We tried the medication route, and that didn't work; then talking to a professional, but in the end, it was Tanya who pulled me back from the dark, and I started to recover. I owe everything to her; she is my angel, my saviour, my love. I know I would kill for her or die for her in equal measure.

'A pint of local best bitter, Martin,' Craig says as I approach him. He hands me one of the pint glasses.

'Spot on, good for starters,' as we smile at each other.

'And I've ordered a wee side just for us,' Craig continues, as the barman places two glasses of single malt whisky beside the first pint on the bar.

Craig hands me one of the whisky glasses and raises his arm slightly, offering up his whisky glass, 'To us, friends for a long time and for a long time to come. Alla nostra!'

'Alla nostra!' and we down the whisky in one go.

'Umm, nice. Shall we join the ladies?'

'Of course,' Craig replies, lead the way, my good man.'

I take a seat beside Tanya, lean in, and give her a small kiss on the cheek. 'Oh, what's that for?'

'Do I need a reason?'

'Of course not, darling,' and she kisses me right back.

'Look at these two,' Craig says to Melissa, 'it's like they're on a first date.'

'Leave them alone; it's nice Martin is showing his wife a little affection, whereas my husband…?'

'Oh, now you've shamed me into it. Come here, wife of mine.' Craig leans into Melissa, and they kiss lightly on the lips. 'There, much better?'

'It's not the same when mentioned to you; a little spontaneity would be welcome, you know. Four years married and you're already slipping, Counsel.'

Craig looks to Martin, 'Now I know I'm in trouble when she's using my official title.' He looks back at Melissa, 'I apologise, Matron.'

'Nurse Practitioner, if you don't mind.'

We all laugh and raise our glasses in a toast.

It's good having friends like these, ones you can rely upon. I know and respect how busy Craig is, but he is always there when needed, helping Tanya source external help when I needed it, often pulling the odd string with friends in higher medical circles.

Tanya took some time off from her career in civil engineering. It was probably not the best time to be away from the office with a couple of large capital projects just starting up, but she did put me first, and I respect and will be eternally grateful for that commitment she made to us.

'So, do they do a Sunday roast here, Martin?' Melissa asks me.

'Oh, sorry, I forgot to ask; I'll check,' and as I rise from the chair, Melissa continues, 'No, it's fine, I was just curious.'

'No, it's alright, I'll check; it seems like a good place for lunch tomorrow before we head back.'

'Great idea,' Craig adds.

I head back to the bar, patiently wait until the barman is free of serving, and get my answer. I reserve a table for four at one p.m., then order another two beers while I have his attention.

Back at the table, I place the two new pints on the tabletop, and Craig, without breaking his conversation with Tanya, acknowledges their arrival with a thumbs up. I turn to Melissa, asking, 'heavy topic of conversation?' nodding to the two of them.

'No, Tanya just made the mistake of asking him about the case he's on and well … you know him, no details but…', she smiles back at me. 'How are you doing Martin? Tanya mentioned you are back writing full time again, that's brilliant.'

'Yes, it is. I lost my way for a bit back then, but I have returned all the stronger for it.'

'So, what's the new book about?'

'It's based around a character who loses everything dear to him through sheer bad luck and misfortune and claws his way back, becoming a stronger, better person, finding his vocation in life and saving himself and others along the way.'

'Whoa, that sounds a little heavy. Is it not a bit close to, well, you know, what you were going through?'

'Not really. I didn't lose everything, but I can relate to that feeling, and it's made me appreciate and hopefully portray it far better than I could have done before. The publishers like it so far, in fact, they are already talking it up somewhat.'

'I don't mean this the wrong way, but are they saying this because it is good or because they want you to believe it's good?'

'Ah, you don't pull any punches, do you.' I can see my reply brought a realisation of what she had just said to me.

'Oh my god, Martin, I didn't mean…'

'No, it's fine, no harm intended or taken. This is what I need. I need people around me who ask awkward questions and challenge the situation. I know you are only watching out for me, and I love that you are confident not to tiptoe around me. No, it really does feel like this is my best work, and my editor has vowed to be plainly honest with me after I asked her to be honest at all times from now on. I don't want another bomb of a book, and they sure as hell don't.'

'Sorry, I can be a bit insensitive at times.'

'It's OK; I wish more people were honest around me; if they had been, that last book wouldn't have nearly been the end of me.'

Melissa leans into me and softly kisses my cheek, whispering 'Sorry' in my ear, and I smile at her as she withdraws.

I enjoyed that kiss; it was nice, comforting, and honest. True friends.

3

Craig – The Wild Boar Inn, Bramblehurst

I sip my beer as I watch the three of them talk of old times and we laugh. Looking at Martin, it's good to see him back to his former self. To be fair, I think we all needed this weekend away, and it couldn't have come at a better time. Tensions and stresses have been coming from all angles over this last year or so. Martin and his mental health issues, with Tanya coping with him and her career at the same time, and Melissa making it to full-time Nurse Practitioner in a newly opened medical centre, and then me, with the case that both excites me and scares me.

The pressures and demands of work have pulled at Melissa and me; we've had some awful rows and the odd few days apart while we each calm down. But we do calm down and come to our senses; we always make it back together and carry on.

My pressure is coming from my current case. A large construction development project comprising restaurants, quality office space and executive apartments overlooking regenerated docklands, a project that failed dramatically last year, involving the loss of tens of millions of pounds of investor's money. There is credible belief that an organised crime group is involved, which is being investigated separately by the police. The dispute I'm involved with, acting on behalf of the Project's Insurers, is to protect the Insurer's position and, thus, the position of their investors. It's not the first time I've acted for Insurers, having built my career on a steady flow of increasingly complex disputes, but it is the first dispute in which I've experienced a personal threat; although proving the threat occurred is near impossible, it'll be viewed as one person's comment to another which is easily refuted as having been misconstrued or misinterpreted by the recipient; however, I do know a threat when I receive one, veiled or not. I won't be swayed; my conscience will direct me, and they are not stupid enough to come after a senior lawyer, are they?

Melissa's new role is more demanding than I expected, but to be fair, she gave me a lot of latitude and support when I was building my career. I am proud of her, but we do have our moments. It's good to see her laughing with Martin and Tanya, and I'm relieved she'll never find out about Tanya and me until I decide the time is right. It was getting serious between Tanya and me, and if I am honest with myself, it was me who instigated things. Martin was in his bad place, and she was feeling lonely and stressed. Melissa was away at a medical conference, which fell on one of those times we were having some time away from each other to calm down. I called at their house and took Tanya out for dinner to help, I thought, escape the everyday humdrum, and then one thing led to another, and we ended up in a hotel room in the city. That first night was probably the most passionate night I have had with anyone, both of us just escaping the world, shedding all the baggage of spouses and careers, and wanting something exciting and daring. It was ludicrous, but it continued for a few weeks until Tanya came to her senses before I did, and she wanted to stop it before anyone got hurt. It was ironic, really, as the two people who were hurt the most were the two of us, but we had to stop it; it was the right thing to do. Martin was starting to improve, and Melissa and I were back together again, and I needed to re-focus my attention on making Partner.

But then, one day, Tanya and I bumped into each other in the city, had a coffee, and it all just restarted, so this weekend, we will need to be very careful.

On the walk this morning, every now and again, I'd catch her looking at me, and, well, that connection is something else. But we're far too sensible to let anything show this weekend; we'd both lose too much if we didn't plan it properly.

'And your thoughts, oh wise one?' Martin's words bringing me back down to earth. 'Hello, anyone in there?'

'Oh, sorry, I was miles away then; thoughts on?'

'See, I said he would be back on his case before the day was out,' Melissa added.

I need to think of something. 'No, I was just watching the three of you, and it reminded me of that holiday we all had in Rhodes a few years back. It was one the best times I have had.'

Martin replies, 'Oh, getting all sentimental, are we? And we've not really got started yet.'

I chuckle slightly, 'If I can't get sentimental about you three, then who can I get all mushy about?'

Melissa reaches across the table, taking my hand. 'My hero, at long last, he's getting in touch with his feminine side.'

We all laugh, and Martin blows me an air kiss, which the couple on the next table see, and we all laugh some more.

'So, my thoughts on what?' I return to, and Martin replies.

'Picking up some food from the village shops this afternoon and heading back to the cottage or dinner out with some drinks this evening?'

'I'm happy with either; I'll go with the flow?'

'Well, that's useful,' says Melissa. 'Honestly, he spends all day making decisions but then can't decide where to eat. I think you'd be lost without me,' she adds and smiles at me.

'I would.' I place my right palm down, flat on the table, 'That's it, dinner out it is then. How's that for a decision?'

'Done,' Martin adds, 'We're escaping domesticity and embracing freedom.'

'And neither of you want to wash the pots, do you?' Tanya quips.

'You know us too well,' I reply to her with a smile and wink, which I sense was received with the underlying message I wanted to send.

4

Tanya – Bramblehurst Forest

Walking through the village, we duck in and out of small shops, not looking for anything in particular, just browsing. I buy some of the local fudge, and Martin and Craig convince us they are in desperate need of some of the locally produced award-winning sausages and free-range eggs for breakfast in the morning, even though we will be having Sunday lunch in The Wild Boar a few hours later.

Melissa and I chat about our workplaces, good offload therapy we call it, as the boys follow behind, talking about sport and politics, which is often dangerous territory for the two of them as their opinions on football teams and politics are polar opposites; *"it's good to debate"* Martin often tells me, *"the food stock a writer needs for inspiration"*. They never come to blows over it, but there have been some heated debates in the past, which frightens both Melissa and me, as we sometimes think they're done, never to speak again, but then they are best buddies again the next day; men do have short memories I suppose.

Leaving the village behind, we climb a stile over a stone wall and walk the public footpath crossing the field towards Bramblehurst Forest; our cottage is just beyond. Well, it's not a cottage; really, it is a converted barn comprising two luxury master bedrooms, with ensuite bathrooms upstairs and a third smaller double bedroom downstairs, towards the rear. The living room boasts a large log-burning fire in the centre of the room and a well-fitted kitchen and dining area, making up the ground floor. And, of course, we have the obligatory hot tub on the patio area overlooking fields and the distant hills. An interior designer has provided the internal décor, that's obvious, but the owner has added one or two of their own touches and a useful, handwritten local guidebook, hence our learning of the footpath cutting through the forest, across the fields, to the village rather than the three-mile drive using country lanes. Leaving the cars behind meant we could enjoy a drink or two at the Inn without any concern.

As we cross the field, we close up and talk about planning a holiday next year, overseas again, as Craig suggests, and we are all in agreement. Craig proposes Rhodes again, and out of the blue, Martin and Melissa both suggest New York, laugh and link arms, then walk ahead like they are pacing out to the airport already. I chip in, 'Madeira', but at this point, only Craig is taking me on.

'Madeira? Now that's interesting. Any reason why?' Craig asks me as he follows suit and offers his arm to link.

Taking his arm, I reply, 'No, not particularly. I read an article a couple of years ago and thought I'd like to visit. Just appeals to me, I suppose.'

'OK, I can buy into that, although those two seem set on New York,' nodding his head forward slightly at Melissa and Martin walking away out in front, locked in conversation about the Big Apple.

Approaching the field boundary and forest beyond, the footpath leads us to a wooden kissing gate. Melissa passes through first, and as she does, she stops on the other side and leans over the gate to Martin, 'It's a called a kissing gate for a reason, you know,' as she closes her eyes and pouts her lips. Martin does not hesitate; he plants a playful kiss on Melissa's lips with a reply, 'So that's the reason, I like it,' as she steps back, and he walks through the gate; then it's our turn. Martin stops, looks over the gate to me, and adopts the same eyes-closed pose but with more overt pouting of the lips.

As I approach him, it's not kissing Martin that is running through my mind; it's the thought that in a few seconds, I'll be placing a kiss on Craig's lips.

Kissing Martin, he pulls away and links up with Melissa again, and they turn to walk off again. I turn to Craig at the gate and see him kneeling, feigning tying his bootlace that hasn't come undone. I know instinctively he's stalling a little, buying some time. Melissa and Martin continue walking away from us, linking arms again, entering the tree line on the muddy path, leaving Craig and me at the gate.

He stands upright and approaches the gate. 'I was hoping we would get a moment to ourselves this weekend, no matter how brief it might be.' He leans over the top of the gate, and we kiss; not a short peck, but a longer kiss, holding our lips together. I can feel the excitement run through me; this is more than two friends clowning around at a kissing gate; this is a deeply passionate kiss, and I just know Craig feels it, too.

'Come on, you two!' Martin shouts from within the trees, 'We're nearly there'.

We break immediately, and I take a step back to let Craig come through the gate. He is smiling, and I smile back at him. In a hushed voice, I say to him, 'We agreed; we have to stay sensible this weekend.'

He links my right arm with his left, smiles warmly, and replies, 'We did, didn't we? What's the harm? We're just two friends walking in the countryside, nothing more than that,' as he closes his arm in tighter to his side, pulling me slightly closer to him, 'Unless you think it differently?' he adds, looking into my eyes.

'No. We agreed, just friends this weekend. OK?'

'But you felt that as well; I know you did.'

'I did, but…'

'I'm enjoying this weekend, the four of us together, but I'd rather it was just the two of us,' he adds.

'Now, come on. That's not fair. We both agreed to be sensible and not put anything at risk.'

'Yes, but that was then, and this is now. Martin is back to his former self, and Melissa is happy now with her career. This should be our time.'

'And what is that supposed to mean? That we can carry on with each other right now, behind their backs?'

'No, I don't mean that, but I do know I want more of you,' and he kisses me on my right cheek. 'And, if you were honest with yourself, you want more of me, don't you?'

My head is screaming, yes, I do, but I know I don't want a sordid secret affair in anonymous hotel rooms anymore. I want more, but that has a price. He knows how I feel about him, and that Melissa is my closest friend, but he's willing to leave Melissa in a heartbeat because that's what he's like; he sets his mind on something and goes for it.

'Craig. Don't be daft, we mustn't; one of them could see us.'

'But we've already started the ball rolling,' he replies quietly.

'You know what I mean.'

'There you are!' Martin calls out. We both look up and forward in his direction and see him about fifteen metres in front at a bend in the path. 'Melissa sent me back to check you're both OK.'

Craig instantly replies, 'Yes, sorry, my bootlace came loose but got knotted. All sorted, we're here now.'

'Good, because we're going to work on you two tonight to agree to New York.'

'Ah, ganging up on us they are,' Craig says to me.

'It seems so,' I reply.

As we turn the bend in the path, I see Melissa in the distance at the far end of the path beyond Martin, standing on top of the timber stile over the stone wall that leads on toward the cottage; the sunlight beyond is silhouetting her against the sky, framed in an archway of trees. There is my best friend, blissfully ignorant of her partner here secretly sleeping with me. It won't be for long; it will all soon change.

5

Martin – Fell View Cottage

Upon returning to the cottage, we all change and climb into the large hot tub, sharing a bottle of champagne even though we know we're not supposed to mix the two. Laughing and joking, we talk of previous weekends away, the fun and troubles we got into and out of, and just how fabulous this cottage is. The hot tub, sheltered from the light wind by the building, provides us with a panoramic view across the valley and up to the peaks of the hills beyond.

It's good us all being back together again. I sorted out my problems, which has put us all back on track again with our careers, lives, and futures. I quite fancy a week in New York, and both Melissa and I agreed to work on them over dinner tonight and keep up the pressure until they crumble.

It's Tanya that brings us back down to earth, 'Well, I'm going in for a shower, then getting ready for dinner this evening.'

'Yeh, I suppose we all better had. Shall we meet at six thirty on the patio for pre-dinner drinks?' Melissa suggests.

'Now that sounds like a plan,' Craig replies, 'six-thirty it is.'

In turns, we step out of the hot tub, grabbing towels and robes. Tanya is the first to enter the cottage and heads for the kitchen area, 'Anyone fancy a cup of tea?' she calls out over her shoulder.

Melissa, following her, 'Yes, please.'

Craig and I look at each other and at the same time say 'Tea?' and we both laugh. I turn to some of the weaponry hanging on the walls and carefully lift down a sword, taking it by the hilt and sweeping it around in mock fencing fashion. Craig follows suit, taking down another sword. We square up to each other, blades crossing, left hands on our hips, and I say in my best French accent, 'En Garde, Monsieur,' we each nod to each other, give the salute, imitating duellists, and then proceed to clatter the blades against each other in a schoolboy pirate kind of way.

On hearing steel on steel, Tanya turns to look at us and shouts, 'Stop it, you bloody fools. You've both been drinking, and they're not toys; they're the real thing, and they're expensive antiques; if the owner finds out, you two will be in a lot of trouble.' Looking at Melissa, she continues shaking her head, 'Bloody men.'

Melissa replies to Tanya, 'They will be if one of them slips with one of those things,' raising her eyebrows and looking at Craig.

Craig and I both stop; he lowers his head and says, 'Sorry, mum.'

'Just put them back where you found them,' Tanya continues before returning to the kettle and cups.

I flick my sword some more in a mock parry followed by a riposte. 'I like the feel of this one; it's well-balanced but robust. Here, try it.'

We swap swords; his sword is lighter, with an ornate engraved Cup Hilt and styled Loop Guards, compared to the sword I took down, which feels like a real battling sword rather than a duelling sword.

Craig re-hangs his sword on the wall, 'Yeh, imagine being in a battle, facing a charging enemy with these; I bet it was terrifying.'

'I suppose it's no worse than somebody half a mile away, that you can't even see, shooting at you or lobbing mortar bombs in your direction.'

'No, I suppose not,' Craig nods in agreement.

As I'm replacing the sword back in its place on the wall, Tanya says she is taking her tea up and will grab a shower as she'll need to dry her hair and Melissa adds, 'Yep, same here. Now play nicely boys. No more swords.' They head upstairs together.

Craig pads barefoot into the kitchen area and opens the refrigerator door, 'Do you fancy a cheeky beer, mate?'

'Yeh, why not? It would be rude not to.'

I pull out a stool at the breakfast bar and fold my towel to sit on it. Craig opens two beer bottles and hands me one, 'Cheers,' we say at the same time as we cross bottlenecks; 'En Garde,' I quip, and we laugh together.

Out of the blue, Craig asks me a question in a rather clumsy way I thought for a lawyer, 'So, are you over all that silliness? Are you all mended now?'

'Well, yes, but I wouldn't call it silliness; it was all very real to me.'

'Yeh, sorry. It's just, erm, I don't think I could get that way, you know.'

His tone is a bit condescending, even for Craig; he was a big help when I went through my bad patch, but he seems a bit different with it now. 'Well, how do any of us know what lies ahead and how we could find ourselves in the future? I wouldn't think it may not happen to you.' His gaze is fixed on his beer bottle, and I take the opportunity to change the subject, 'Are you worried about that threat you mentioned earlier?'

'Yeh, I suppose I am a bit. Sorry, work pressures and all, I'll be fine when we get a couple of these current cases resolved.'

'Well, that kind of threat would be enough to get anyone stressed.'

'Maybe I'll take one of these swords home with me for protection,' he jokes, and we tap bottles again.

'Have you mentioned it to Melissa?'

He looks back at his beer bottle, 'Yes and no. I mentioned to her the other week about being more diligent, keeping an eye open for anything out of the ordinary, be aware of anyone unusual or suspicious, and she started to freak a little, so I toned it down; I definitely didn't mention it was a clear threat, I just said it's the kind of thing a new Partner gets advised about, risks of the job you know, and she kind of accepted it.'

'Ah, OK. Then I won't say anything to Tanya, as she will only mention it to Melissa.'

'Cheers, yeh, keep it between us.' We both take a long pull on our beers.

'Do you know who it is that has threatened you?'

'Yes and no, I can't prove who I think it is, but I'd be surprised if I'm wrong.'

'Who is it? Can you tell me?'

'I shouldn't; the police told me not to say anything, as if it is a serious threat, they could act it out.'

'Jeez, and I bet that spooked you?'

'Yes, it bloody did.' He's playing with his beer bottle, picking at the label with a fingernail. 'Look between us, just in case something was to happen, I think it originated from someone senior in the Costas family, a large, Greek family-owned construction and development company involved in all kinds of projects around the country. They are well connected but have some money problems from what I've heard.'

'Oh right, hence the need to get the hundred million pay settlement.'

Looking up at me with a serious expression, 'Yep. Keep this between us, yeh?'

'Yes, of course, no problem. I'll not say anything to anyone.'

Craig puts his almost empty bottle down on the breakfast bench. 'Right, I suppose we had best go up and show willing.'

'Yep, we're already in the bad books over the swordplay,' we nod to each other with raised eyebrows and smiles.

'No change there then,' he adds.

Entering the bedroom, Tanya is still in the shower, so I grab my canvas Messenger bag and hop up onto the bed. Propping myself up on the collection of pillows against the headboard, I take out my small notebook, which I keep handy to capture thoughts and ideas for my writing and jot down a few thoughts while they are still fresh in my head. My notes follow the conversations earlier today and the one just with Craig, jotting out the outline of the threat he has received from a senior person in a large construction company that needs his law firm to acknowledge an insurance payout. I don't write down the company name in case someone reads my notes. He is trying to brush it to one side, but I can see he is troubled by it, and it's clearly on his mind with that flip comment about taking a sword home with him for protection. Asking him outright if the threat is credible, he clearly thinks it is, saying he could see why the threat had been made if the Insurers didn't pay out on the one hundred-million-pound policy, and he is in a prominent position currently to decide if the claim is legitimate under the policy or not, the fourth-generation family business will probably go bankrupt; but naturally, the Insurers would like the sizeable claim to be rejected and need his expertise to find technical points in the policy terms and conditions. He mentioned he thought the development project involved organised crime investors and no doubt the payout would be more about them getting their money back than protecting the family business. To me, this seems like good information to base a crime thriller around, and I'm eagerly jotting notes and comments based on what Craig mentioned, outlining a potential story plan.

Lowering my notebook to my lap, I look around the room and then at the bed; it's enormous, super king size, with white Egyptian cotton sheets and six pillows further peppered with cushions and throws. Tanya loves this kind of decor. It's amazing; I feel so different from this time last year; it's like I am a new person, liberated of the iron shackles trying to drown me as I frantically swim to the shore, shackles that were pulling me deeper and further away. Just the simple act of writing down ideas and thoughts for another book is a huge step forward and one I thought I would never take again, or at least not for a very long time. Tanya has been and is my saviour; she taught me how to release those shackles so I could swim freely again.

My illness must have been tough on her. I couldn't see it then, but I can now, and I now appreciate she was in a difficult place with the pressures of her work and me, sinking deeper and deeper into oblivion, but she did it; she stood by me in my hour of need, and I will be forever grateful for her love and support. Her employers were sympathetic in the end, but only following the ultimatum, she felt forced to level with them, that she needed the time off or she would leave.

Tanya walks into the bedroom from the ensuite, wrapped in a large white robe and her hair wrapped in a towel like a turban. 'Oh good, what are you writing?'

"Just some notes on something Craig mentioned today. I think they would be good material to base a book on.'

'Ah, and does Craig get a share of the royalties?' she asks, smiling at me.

'To be honest, I don't think he will want to know the outcome of this story when I finish it.'

'Ah, another thriller then, with a twist of murder.'

'Something like that.'

'You'd best wrap that up for now and grab a shower. We're meeting downstairs for drinks in thirty minutes.'

'OK, no probs.' I close my notebook, and as I'm placing it on the bedside table, I say to Tanya without looking at her, 'You two seemed quite pally today, quite close.'

'Who, me and Melissa? We always are.'

'No, you and Craig.'

'Really? It's funny that I was thinking that of you and Melissa; planning a trip to New York had you both in a world of your own.'

Turning to look at her, she is standing with hands on hips, shaking her head from side to side, and smiling at me.

OK, she's got me there, 'Touché.'

6

Craig – Fell View Cottage

Dinner tonight was good fun; the food was simple but honest and well prepared, with wine and beer free flowing, although the idea of walking back through the fields in the dark afterwards with a single pocket torch between us was probably not thought through fully. That said, the ladies hold tight to Martin and me, especially after each fox howl and bark carried on the night breeze. The clear night sky hosts a canopy of stars over us, and just outside the cottage, we sit for a few minutes on the patio chairs, heads craned backwards, taking in the sheer enormity of the night sky.

Martin whispers something to Tanya, stands and enters the cottage. Through the sliding glass doors, I watch him set the fire and then light the log burner; not that it is cold, more for atmosphere setting I suppose. Melissa and Tanya follow him in when they see the flames build. I decide to remain outside for now, in the peace of the countryside, with no town light pollution spoiling the night sky and no traffic noise or sirens. After a few minutes, Melissa opens the sliding patio door, steps out and closes it behind her. She has two wine glasses in her left hand, cupped between her fingers.

'Is one of those for me?'

'Yes, of course,' she replies, 'When have you known me to drink red wine?' handing the glass of Rioja to me.

'Thank you, and never. It's times like these I wonder whether we have the right partners.'

Sipping her white wine, she splurts a little for effect more than anything and replies, 'Really?'

I chuckle, 'No, I don't mean anything by that; it's just that you and Martin only drink white wine, and Tanya and I only drink red. That's all. If we drank the same wine, we probably wouldn't drink as much, as we'd be sharing the same bottle.'

'Yeah, right; you'd still drink just as much; it would just be two bottles of the same opened. I know you too well.'

'Yes, you're probably right.'

Melissa pulls up one of the wooden chairs beside me, sits and looks upward. 'It is lovely, isn't it?'

'Yes,' I reply, deep sighing, 'it really is.'

'Why the sigh, are you not happy here?'

'Yes, I am. No, I'm just slowing my breathing, enjoying the company and the night, but I am a realist; I'll be back at my desk on Monday morning and back into that bloody claim.'

'I thought you were enjoying it. Enjoying the challenge?'

'I am. It's just… no, it doesn't matter, it can wait.'

'Good. That's it, put it to one side, it's not here with us this weekend. Let's enjoy what we have now.' We clink our glasses together and sip our wine.

A few minutes later, Tanya pulls the door aside, 'Are you two staying out there or coming in and trying some of these cheeses we bought today?'

'We're coming,' Melissa replies. Looking at me, 'Come on,' as she taps my thigh, 'Let's go join the party.'

We both stand and walk in through the patio doors, and I pull the door across to close it. Melissa joins Tanya at the table, selecting some of the cheeses, grapes, and chutneys foraged today from the village shops.

Martin is putting on some music in the background, and we tuck in and drink more wine.

7

Martin – Fell View Cottage

Early Sunday Morning, 11th June

Boom! Boom! Boom! Whoa, my head! Opening my eyes, the sunlight entering the bedroom sears into my skull. How much did we drink last night? I turn my head ever so slowly to my left to look at Tanya, but she's not there. In fact, it doesn't look like she came to bed; her side of the bed is undisturbed.

Boom! Boom! Boom! It's downstairs. Someone is banging on the cottage door, sounding very insistent. I sit up and swing my legs out of bed and go to stand, but stumble as I put my weight on them. 'Jeez, that was some party,' I say out loud. 'Tanya. Are you in the bathroom?' squinting my eyes in a feeble attempt to restrict light and headache. There's no reply.

I stagger over to the sash window and look out and down towards the door. There are police, lots of them. Lifting the sash window open, I call down to them and instantly wish I hadn't; the pain in my head is well up on the scale of one to ten.

'Can you open the door please, Sir?'

'Is that a question or an instruction?'

'An instruction, open the door now, please.'

'Why?'

'Open the door now, please, Sir, or we'll have no choice but to force it open.'

There is a shout from below but to my left. 'Sarge, the patio door is unlocked. Shall I go in?'

He turns to look in the direction the voice came from, 'Yes, wait. I'm coming with you. You stay here,' he orders one of the other officers, 'No one comes in until I say. Got it?'

'Yes, Sarge.'

Bloody hell, 'What the f...,' I turn quickly and lose my balance, falling toward the dressing table; reaching out, I grab hold of the tabletop but just sufficient to deflect my fall away from it, and I land on the sheepskin rug with a thud.

"*What the...*" to myself, "*get a grip, Marty boy, you've drunk far more than that in the past. Come on; something is happening downstairs. Get up, you lightweight.*"

I stand again, but I'm still unsteady on my feet. I walk around the bed to the door, using furniture and the wall for support, and when I open it, I hear multiple voices downstairs. I look to my left, down the landing, towards Craig and Melissa's bedroom. Seeing their door closed, I stagger out onto the landing and look down over the balcony rail to the living room area. I see three police officers, one coming up the stairs towards me.

'The police Sergeant looks up at me, 'Are you alone, Sir?'

'Err, no, my wife and our friends are here. What's going on?'

The Sergeant shouts up to the Constable, 'Walker! Round them up and bring them down here.'

'Yes, Sarge,' he replies as he approaches me.

'What's going on, Officer?'

'Sir, can you and your wife come downstairs, please? Your friends are in that room there, are they, Sir?' as the Officer points past me to the door at the end of the landing.

'Yes. Craig and Melissa.'

'OK, thank you, Sir. Please, if you wouldn't mind coming downstairs with your wife?'

'Er, yes, of course, but Tanya, my wife, must already be downstairs; she's not in here or the bathroom.'

'Thank you,' he replies, motioning I should go downstairs.

'I'll just put a robe on.' Grabbing a white robe from the back of the door, I pull it on and fasten the tie at my waist, then make my way to the stairs. As I start to descend, observed by another police constable, I come over all light-headed and stagger again, gripping the handrail hard to steady myself.

'Are you OK, sir?' the Officer asks.

'Yes, just a little too much to drink last night, I think, although I don't recall drinking that much.'

The Sergeant is waiting patiently for me, standing in the middle of the living room, hands on his hips.

Squinting, I walk towards the man in charge, 'What's all this about, Sergeant? Why are you here?'

'Your name first, please, Sir.'

'Martin Nicholson.'

'And your wife?'

'Tanya. She must be down here or outside; she's not upstairs.'

'Nicholson also?'

'Er, yes… my wife, I did say.'

'Not all wives take their husband's names these days, Sir.'

'Yes, well, I suppose so,' rubbing both temples with the tips of my fingers. 'So, what is it? A noise complaint? Seems a bit heavy handed wanting to crash the door in, don't you think?'

The Constable upstairs comes to the landing rail and calls down, 'Sarge, there's only one up here, a female. I can't wake her. I think we need an ambulance fast.'

'Stay calm, Walker; remember your training. ABC.'

'Sarge?'

'Airway, Breathing, Circulation.'

'Yes, Sarge, I've done that. She is breathing, and she has a pulse, but I can't wake her.'

'Smith, get a paramedic here pronto; tell them it's my request.'

'Yes, Sarge.'

'It'll be Melissa; we drank quite a bit last night,' I try to explain to the Sergeant.

He remains formal, 'Now, Sir, full names of your friends, if you please?'

'Craig and Melissa, both with the surname Tyler.'

'Now you're getting it. And where are they at the moment?'

'Well, I thought they were both upstairs in their bedroom.'

Whilst jotting down notes, the Sergeant calls out, 'Smith. How are you doing with that paramedic?'

'About ten minutes away, Sarge.'

'Good, Walker. Keep an eye on the lady upstairs until the paramedic gets here.' He turns to me, 'What's in that room there, sir?' pointing to the door at the back of the cottage beyond the kitchen area.

'Another bedroom. It's empty, just a spare.'

'Smith, Dhawan; take a look in there, will you.'

'Yes, Sarge.'

'You haven't said why you're here, Sergeant.'

'No, I haven't; I'll explain in a minute.'

I look past the Sergeant to the two uniformed officers as they knock on the door, announce their presence as police officers, then enter the third bedroom. I hear the female Officer say out loud 'shit' and run in after her colleague, then shouting back, 'Sarge. They're in here!'

'Wait here, Sir,' the Sergeant instructs me. 'Don't go anywhere.'

'Like, where would I go?' I reply, but he is already heading to the bedroom door. My head is pounding, and I feel nauseous, but I need to find out what's going on. I walk closer to the bedroom and hear the Sergeant query, 'Dead? Both of them?'

'Yes, Sarge,' the female Officer replies. 'It's like she said, she heard it right.'

'OK, don't touch anything; outside, you two, seal the room and take Mr Nicholson out to the car. I'll call it in.'

The Sergeant reappears from the bedroom, and the female Officer walks around him and approaches me. 'Please, sir, follow me out to the car.' I look at her as she beckons me towards the front door.

Unsure of what is going on but concerned over the words "*both of them are dead*", I turn to the Sergeant. 'I think you need to explain what is going on here, Sergeant. Bursting in like this, no explanation, someone's dead, and now you're telling me I have to go outside and sit in a police car. What is this about? Who is dead?'

His reply is curt and forceful: 'Please, Sir. Outside now with my Officer and wait in the car.'

'No! For god's sake, what the hell is going on here?'

He squares up to me, taking a step forward. 'There are two deceased persons in that room, and their deaths are suspicious. Now, I'll ask you one more time to wait outside in the car whilst we seal this building for senior officers and the CSI team, or I will arrest you.'

If it's Melissa upstairs that they've called the paramedics for, then… 'Oh my god, Tanya!' I try to go past the Sergeant, but he quickly blocks my path and takes hold of me.

'Smith! Get him outside now! Dhawan, assist him.'

Both police officers acknowledge the order in unison, 'Yes, Sarge,' and they each take a hold of my arms and try to direct my moving towards the front door.

'No! No!' You're not taking me outside; get off me! Tanya! Tanya!'

'Get him outside now! Use restraints if needs be.'

I'm jostled to the front door, and the male police officer tries to open it. However, the heavy iron slide bolt is across the door, locked into the door jamb. As he goes to lift the bolt handle and draw the bolt back, the Sergeant shouts out.

'Stop. Take him out via the patio doors; leave that door bolted.'

As they turn me towards the patio doors at the far end of the living room, the Sergeant changes his instruction. 'No, wait.' He deep sighs, 'Go ahead, unbolt the door, go out that way; it's obvious no one has used that door since it was bolted shut. There could be forensics by the patio door; they were unlocked when we got here, and we don't want to contaminate any evidence. Get him in the car, and Dhawan, secure the patio door and area outside.'

I look back over my shoulder at the Sergeant, seeing him reaching for his personal radio fastened to his left shoulder and I try one last time, 'What's going on?'

'It looks like a double murder, Sir.'

'Murder?'

'Now get him outside, and Smith, stay with him in the car.'

The male police officer responds in the affirmative; they unlock the front door and move me outside to one of the police cars parked on the shingle driveway, bundling me into the back seat and closing the door behind me.

8

Martin – Mylesham Police Station

I've been sitting here in the interview room for nearly half an hour now, dressed in nothing but a white paper boiler suit and cheap disposable slip-on shoes. A police officer stands beside the door, watching over me. No one has told me who is dead, but I am thinking it must be Tanya and Craig, although I'm selfishly hoping that it's Melissa and that Tanya just slept in the other bedroom last night, but I can't see how that would have happened; I just can't remember what happened last night.

I can recall the meal at the pub, the walk back across fields and through the woods, getting back to the cottage and us all starting on wine and cheeses, putting on some music, laughing; then, that's it, that is all I can remember. I said all this to the Detective Inspector I spoke with after stripping off my clothes and putting on this stupid garment. He assured me that I was not under arrest or caution and was merely helping them with their enquiries; the garments are needed for forensics to rule me out from other samples being collected. But he still would not tell me who was at the hospital and who was dead; he said he wasn't able to provide identities just yet, only that a male and female were dead and that a female was in hospital but not in a good way. I think I made him angry when I banged the table, and I said I could make the identifications in less than three seconds, and if I'm helping with enquiries, then he should let me do it. That's when he left the room, leaving me here to stew and worry.

A Detective Sergeant then appeared and asked if I would consent to provide a blood sample and mouth swab for DNA analysis, both of which I provided, and I've been waiting ever since.

Looking up at the police officer by the door, 'Is there any chance I can get a glass of water or a cup of tea?'

He looks at me without moving his body position, 'I can get that for you in a minute or two, Sir, when the DI comes back.'

I sigh, and he looks straight ahead again, disinterested in me.

I can hear footsteps in the corridor, then some shallow, mumbled voices just as the door opens. The DI and DS both walk into the room and straight away ask the young Officer for three cups of tea; he nods his head and leaves the room. The DI and DS take a seat opposite me and place a folder and a laptop on the table. The DS opens a notebook, but the DI keeps the A4 size file closed, and he speaks first.

'We're sorry to keep you waiting, Mr Nicholson. We had some preliminary enquiries and checks to make before we could provide you with more information.'

'I'm getting really frustrated that I'm isolated in here, and you haven't told me anything of any real substance yet other than there are two people dead and one in hospital. Well? What's happened?' Who… who is dead?'

'I'm sorry to inform you, Sir, we believe the deceased female to be your wife, Tanya Nicholson, and the deceased male is one,' briefly looking inside the file, 'one Craig Tyler, who I understand was a close personal friend of you and your wife; is that correct?'

I know I'm just staring at him, trying to take in what he has just said to me. He is talking but I'm not hearing him. Lowering my shaking head into my hands, I kind of already expected this, but I didn't want it to be true.

'Mr Nicholson?'

Tanya's dead. Craig is Dead. Melissa is in hospital. Still shaking my head, I mumble into my hands, 'What happened?'

'That's what we intend to establish, Mr Nicholson.'

'How… how did they die?' I manage to stutter out.

'We are treating their deaths as suspicious, and any information you can provide will be of enormous help, Mr Nicholson. Can I call you Martin?'

'Er, yes, whatever.'

'Thank you. Now, Martin, was there any ill feeling between you, your wife, or you and Craig Tyler? Any fall out or incident that you wish to share with us?'

I look up at him, 'Why are you asking me that?'

'We are simply gathering as much information as we can, Martin. Is there anything that may have a bearing on this matter?'

'You're treating their deaths as suspicious. Were they murdered?'

The DS looks to the DI, who nods slightly. The DS speaks up, 'Yes, Martin, we believe they were murdered.'

The DI steps back in, adding, 'We know they were murdered, Martin, there is no doubt about that. We need your account of your movements after you all returned to the cottage last night.'

'I've already told you all I can remember. We were having a good time, then your Officers were banging on the door this morning; I can't remember what happened in between.' I drop my head again to my hands, inhale, pause, and then look up at the DI, 'Do you think I did this? That I killed them? Oh my god, do I need a solicitor?'

'No, Martin. We don't think that, but if you would like a solicitor present, that is your right. You're not under caution, but we can arrange a solicitor for you if you like. Would you like a solicitor present?'

Looking again at them sitting opposite me, my reply is short: 'Er, yes, I think I do.' The DS and DI look at each other, nod slightly, and stand. As the DI picks up the folder, he asks, 'Do you have a solicitor in mind, or would you like us to arrange a duty solicitor?'

'I… I… I don't know. Erm… I don't know a solicitor, so… yes, a duty solicitor will do, I think.'

'OK, we'll arrange for one to be with you shortly,' the DI replies just as the door opens, and the uniformed police officer tries to enter with three plastic cups of tea on a small tray.

The DS and DI both lift a cup from the tray, and the DI nods to the Officer to give me the remaining cup.

I look up at them in the doorway, 'How did they die?'

'We are holding on to that information for the time being, Martin. We'll get you that solicitor sorted,' and they both leave the room, closing the door behind them, leaving me with the uniformed officer and a plastic cup of tea.

9

Martin – Mylesham Police Station

Just as I finish my second cup of tea, following two cups of water, the door opens, and a woman walks in. She is wearing a dark two-piece trouser suit, a little dishevelled, spectacles perched high on her head, and a battered open briefcase tucked under her arm, the top-opening type that an old schoolmaster would carry.

'Martin Nicholson?' holding out her right hand, 'I'm Kaja Wójcik, duty solicitor. I believe you've requested legal representation?'

I stand and push forward my hand to greet hers, 'Yes, yes, I have, although I'm not sure why.'

'That is not a problem. Is this the first time you've been in a police station?'

'Yes, I mean no. I reported some car damage a few years ago, but certainly, this is the first time I've been in the back of a police station.'

'OK,' she says as she pulls out one of the plastic chairs, sits down, and places her briefcase beside it. 'First, my card,' she hands me her business card. 'Now, what do you know of this incident?'

I look at the card and reply, 'Not a great deal. The Detective Inspector said my wife and my friend have been murdered, and my other friend is in hospital.' Looking up at her, I see her eyes are locked on me.

'That'll be Detective Inspector Robbins?'

'Er. Yes, that's him.'

'Right. I'm sorry to confirm this, but yes, it is as DI Robbins has indicated. Your wife and Mr Tyler have been murdered, and your other friend, Melissa Tyler, is in hospital.'

Hearing her words, I just break down and start to cry, sobbing deeply and moaning quietly. It's hitting me now; the enormity of the situation is sinking in. She reaches inside her briefcase, removes a small packet of tissues, extracts one and hands it to me. 'I'm very sorry, Mr Nicholson.'

I sniff loudly, inhaling, trying to calm myself. Taking the tissue, I wipe my eyes and then blow my nose. She still has her eyes locked on me as I look at her and ask, 'What do you know? The police are not telling me much.'

'I have nothing further about their deaths, but it seems you are the prime suspect.'

'Me? Why? But it's my Tanya and my friend Craig that have been killed, and my friend, Melissa, is in hospital.'

'Yes, quite.'

'I didn't do this! How dare they think I did!'

'Please, you must remain calm. I think that is why the police are keeping their options open with you, playing it by the book, as statistically, violence in a domestic setting is often by a spouse or close partner, and you fulfil those categories, you have survived this ordeal, along with your friend's wife who is in hospital and cannot be interviewed yet; so you are the only one they can talk with at this time.'

'What about Melissa? How is she? Is she injured?'

She reaches down into her briefcase and pulls out a thin card folder and an A4-size writing pad. Looking at the notes, she reads aloud, 'It is thought Melissa is suffering from acute alcohol poisoning; she is being treated currently. She is expected to recover, although the extent of any lasting damage is yet to be determined.'

'Can I see her?'

'I'll see what I can do, but I expect that DI Robbins will block it at this time; he will want to speak to her before you do. Now, let's get some details and prepare a statement in case we have to go on the record. I expect you will be formally interviewed soon.'

'I've already been interviewed.'

'Formally? On tape, under caution?'

'No, they said I was helping with their enquiries.'

'Ah, OK, leave that with me; DI Robbins should know better than that.'

'Let's run through what you can remember, and then we'll prepare that statement. When the interview starts, after confirming your name, etcetera, I strongly recommend you only reply with "no comment"; it'll be in your interest.'

'Won't that make me look guilty, like I have something to hide?'

'Well, until you can recall what happened or the police piece this together, I would say "no comment" is your safest position at this time.'

'It does look bad, doesn't it? I have to convince the police I didn't do this, so saying no comment won't help.' I pause for a second and look at her closely. Do you think I did it?'

'It's not my position to think about that. I'm here to make sure you receive appropriate legal guidance and advice and that the police act properly.'

I'm not convinced by her answer; she thinks I did it as well.

10

DI Robbins – Mylesham Police Station

In my office, preparing notes for the interview, I mull over a strategy to adopt. Martin Nicholson: umm, he doesn't seem like the kind of guy to commit a crime like this. Clean record, model citizen, successful published author; from initial interviews of people who knew the four of them, they were all really good friends. Even the landlord at The Wild Boar Inn has said they were jolly, friendly, having a good time yesterday, dropping in for a few drinks in the afternoon and then returning in the evening for dinner, even reserving a table for Sunday lunch the next day; they were the perfect patrons, even to leaving a decent tip for the serving team after dinner.

But we have his prints on the door to the third bedroom and on the murder weapon, admittedly along with others, and naturally, I'm sure we'll find traces of him on his wife's body and possibly on the other victim, Craig. The thing that is bugging me though, is the patio door being unlocked; it would give access to anyone who tried the door. Again, we have Martin's prints on the patio door handle, along with others, but that's easily explainable. If there is another person involved, then this is their likely entry and exit route.

CSI has taken dozens of samples and prints from the bedroom, living room, kitchen, patio entrance, and garden area. They have also picked up many boot prints around the garden area of varying sizes and tread types. However, a lot of this, if not all of it, could easily be previous occupants, the owners, or maintenance personnel; we'll have to eliminate them all, and this will be costly and time-consuming.

The other person of interest, Melissa, is now stable in hospital but remains unconscious, recovering from excessive alcohol intake to the extent of alcohol poisoning. I suspect she will probably be of little help to us, but she will need to be interviewed. Currently, she is blissfully unaware of her husband's death, unaware of his murder, along with that of her friend, on the basis that she wasn't involved, that is and wasn't trying to drink herself to death after they were murdered.

We need to formally identify the two victims, but they do match the driving licence details in their personal belongings found in the cottage.

I'll need to tread carefully with Martin. My gut is telling me he is another victim in all this. However, he could easily be the killer, especially with his prints on the murder weapon, and maybe he just thought to leave the patio door unlocked to make it look like an intruder was present; I'll need to probe for a motive. The obvious motive, if it was him, is jealousy. The two victims were clearly in a sexual relationship; maybe he knew about the relationship, even consenting or acquiescing to start with, but then struggled with it, or perhaps he had only just found out about them and killed them in a rage. There was no blood found on him, and although the sword has his prints on the handle, there are prints from unidentified others as well.

OK, I'm going push him; let's see if his anger will lower his guard. It's a hard line to take, especially if he's innocent, losing his wife and friend like that, but it isn't the first domestic murder I've done, and no doubt it won't be the last. Standing, collecting my papers together, I walk into the open plan incident room and shout across the floor to my DS, 'Is his solicitor here yet, Colin?' He raises his head above the computer screen on his desk.

'Yes, Boss. Arrived about twenty minutes ago.'

'Good. Come on. They've had long enough together. Let's get this interview underway.'

'Yes, Boss.'

As I walk past desks, I give instructions to various detectives and uniformed officers to chase this and check that, and they all acknowledge their actions. We all know that the first twenty-four to forty-eight hours are crucial in cases like this, and we need to be on our game. The DCI will be hounding me shortly for an update, not happy that his Sunday golf game will have been interrupted with news of a double murder on his patch. I need to give him something positive that he can take to the Chief – we're all just a part of that great big food chain, I suppose.

'C'mon, Holt, chop chop, time and tide and all that.'

He replies, 'Here, Boss,' and I hear him trotting up behind me.

'I'll take the lead, you follow. I'm going to shake him a little and see what falls from the tree. You keep an eye on his body language, got it?'

'Yes, Boss. You think he did this?'

'I'm not sure yet, but he is my prime suspect at the moment.'

We turn the corner, open the doors, and descend a floor to the interview rooms.

Walking past the duty Sergeant, standing at his high desk behind a perspex screen, I see him punching the keyboard with both index fingers. Looking at him as

I slow down a little, 'Morning Terry, which room for Nicholson?'

'Morning Sir, Interview Room One. His solicitor is with him; it's Ball Buster.'

'Oh, great. Cheers.'

We walk into the room, and Martin is sitting with Kaja. Both look up at us.

'Good morning, Miss Wójcik; I trust you are well?'

'Yes, thank you, Detective Inspector.' She looks at Colin as he walks in behind me. 'Good morning, Colin. Are the children well?'

'Morning Miss Wójcik, yes, they are, thank you, for what little I see of them these days, that is,' he replies.

Taking the chairs opposite Martin and Kaja, I place my folder on the table while DS Holt checks the audio recorder; I take the opportunity to be civil.

'Would you like some refreshments, Martin? Miss Wójcik?' Tea or coffee?' They both decline, and I continue. 'This is an informal interview, and we appreciate your assistance. This interview will be recorded. I presume your solicitor has advised you of your rights.'

Martin replies, 'Yes, she has.'

'Good. When we start, I will advise you that you are under caution.'

Martin swiftly turns his head to Kaja, and she speaks quietly to him, advising him this is standard procedure and to remember what they had discussed; he nods and looks back at me.

DS Holt pushes the recorder button, and it beeps continuously. I raise my palms up to show that I am waiting before speaking and lower them when the beep stops.

'Good morning,' I say, quickly looking at my watch. 'Sorry, good afternoon. The time is fourteen twenty-two on Sunday, the eleventh of June. This is the first recorded interview with Mr Martin Nicholson. I am Detective Inspector Paul Robbins, West Ryshire Constabulary, and I'm accompanied by my colleague…'

'Detective Sergeant Colin Holt.'

'Present also is Mr Martin Nicholson and his solicitor.' I look at Nicholson, 'Please say your full name and address for the recording.'

'Yes, er, Martin Edward Nicholson, The Studio, 12 The High Street, Northampton.'

'And Mr Nicholson is represented by duty solicitor…'

'Miss Kaja Wójcik.'

'Thank you. Mr Nicholson, you have consented to this voluntary interview?'

'Yes, I have.'

'Thank you. I must advise you this interview will be conducted under caution. You do not have to say anything. But it may harm your defence if you do not mention when questioned something which you later rely on in court. Anything you do say may be given in evidence. Do you understand this caution?'

He flashes a brief look at Kaja, who nods, and he replies, 'Yes.'

'OK, thank you.' But before I move on, Ball Breaker steps in.

'Detective Inspector. Firstly, I would like to put on record that you have already spoken with my client without legal representation present and without putting my client under caution.'

'That is correct, Miss Wójcik. My colleagues and I conducted a preliminary discussion to establish some basic facts as we were unsure who the deceased persons were in relation to your client and what important information your client could provide that may have been of immediate help in catching the person responsible for this heinous crime.'

'Noted. However, you are aware of the correct procedure, I take it?' she asks.

'Yes, I am, thank you for reminding me.' She just had to get that on tape, didn't she? She never misses an opportunity to capture due process steps on tape.

Miss Wójcik continues. 'My client is willing to assist you with your inquiries. However, should your questions risk prejudicing my client's interest and his intent to assist you, my client reserves his right not to comment. Is that understood?'

'Yes, of course Miss Wójcik.' I'll have to go slowly, or she'll close this down before I get started. I look to her client, 'Mr Nicholson, may I call you Martin?'

'Yes, of course.'

'Thank you. Martin, please describe your movements yesterday, last evening and this morning, in your own words, up to the point my officers entered the cottage early this morning?'

'Yes, but I've already gone through this with one of your officers when I was sitting in a police car outside the cottage before I got here.'

'Yes, I am aware of that and thank you. But we would like to capture this on tape and then have you make a formal written statement.'

'Sure, anything that will help catch the person that did this.'

For the next quarter of an hour, Martin talks more or less non-stop through the events leading up to this weekend break, through yesterday and last night, to this morning. He seems pretty lucid but at times upset, on the verge of tears, most notably when he mentions his wife's name. I watch him carefully, as no doubt my colleague is also. He appears genuine and sincere and does not hold back on any of the timeline that I can see, that is, up to the point where he has no further recollection until being woken by police officers banging on the front door of the cottage.

'Thank you, Martin. Now, I'm going to ask you some questions, and I would like you to answer them as clearly and fully as you can.'

'Yes, but before we go any further, can I ask how Tanya and Craig died?'

DS Holt looks at me, and I at him. Assuming Martin is innocent, he has a right to know, and it will all come out in the fullness of time anyway.

'Yes, of course. Now, I am not going to reveal all the details just yet as we want to retain some key points that only the killer will know. I'm sure you can appreciate this.'

'Er, yes, I can. But was it quick?'

'We believe so. However, this can only be confirmed by the Pathologist following the postmortem examination.'

'A postmortem?' He mumbles as he lowers his head into his hands.

'I'm sorry, Martin, a postmortem examination is essential in such crimes.' He looks devastated when I say this.

Kaja places her right hand on his left arm and looks at me, tilting her head ever so slightly.

'Would you like a glass of water, Martin?

He sniffs, wiping his eyes with his fingers dragging across his face and looks at me. 'So, how did they die?'

I am determined to hold some information back for the time being, but I do need to answer this question as we are on tape, and he could be that innocent victim. I phrase my response to generate a reaction from him.

'Martin, they were in bed together. It is clear that they were in a sexual relationship.'

'NO!' he shouts out, slamming both hands down hard on the table. 'No, I don't believe you. My wife and my friend? Never!'

His reaction is interesting. 'Now, Martin, I recognise this will be upsetting for you, but I ask that you remain calm.'

Miss Wójcik interjects, 'If we could have five minutes, please, Detective Inspector, to let my client regain his composure? You clearly provided some upsetting news to my client.'

I look at Colin and nod. 'Yes, of course. Interview suspended at… fourteen forty-three.' Colin stops the machine. 'We'll get you that water.'

Outside the room, we look at each other, speaking quietly, 'What do you think, Colin? Did he do it?'

'I'm not sure. One minute, he seems fine, clear, and in control; the next, he's upset. It could be he recalls what he has done and is full of remorse, or he is completely innocent.'

'There could be a love triangle thing here, I suppose, the manner in which they were killed indicates a rage, a vengeful act, but almost a spur-of-the-moment thing. It doesn't feel planned in advance; the murder weapon was already at the scene; a professional would have come equipped with a weapon of choice if it was planned.'

'I agree with you there, Boss. But this guy? I just don't know; I don't think he has it in him.'

'Well, he flipped quickly then. Do any of us know what we are capable of until that button is pushed?'

'I guess not, but I'd hope I'm not capable of doing what this killer did.'

'No, it was quite brutal. Can you get that water arranged? We'll go back in shortly. I'll just pop upstairs and check with the team, see if anything new has come up.'

'Yes, Boss, will do.'

11

DI Robbins – Mylesham Police Station

Walking upstairs to the Incident Room, I play over the interview in my head, and whilst we can place him at the murder scene and his prints are on the murder weapon and, we possibly have a motive of jealousy or rage, it just doesn't feel like he did it. That said, the only thing going in his favour is the unlocked patio door and, I suppose, the lack of any blood traces on him or his clothes from the two victims.

He has a memory gap, though, and I need to understand why. This could have been done in a blind rage, and he just can't recall it, bringing in some form of temporary instability or a psychological after-effect following the murders when his conscious side is blocking the horror of his actions, detaching, and disowning them. I think we may need a professional to assess his state of mind.

Opening the door, I see everyone is busy on phones, radios, and computer screens. One of the new probationary Detective Constables is at the end of the room, adding photos and notes to the crime board. I walk slowly through the room, listening but not disturbing, mindful that if anyone has anything for me, they will let me know. All in this room know how I work; if it's important, they must bring it to me personally. I'm not having any hierarchical nonsense filtering information or any individual's brown-nosing; in my experience, it's often the smallest point that can turn a case, so I need to know everything.

I reach the bottom of the room, standing outside my office door, making sure I have made eye contact with each officer, so they know I'm here, waiting for information they are mining. Looking over at the crime board, I see photos of the two victims in happier times alongside some of the more graphic scene of crime photos. The graphic images are not appropriate for general consumption, and I wander over and start removing them. The young DC turns her head to me, 'Sorry, Sir, should they not be on the Board?'

'No, I think not. There are some details we want to keep between us and the killer, so the fewer that know about them, the better. Plus, I don't want to be looking at a scene like that every hour, as grotesque but intriguing as it is.'

'OK, sorry, Sir, I was told to put some of the crime scene photos up.'

'Sorry, remind me of your name again.'

'Hansen, Sir. Joanna Hansen.'

'OK Joanna, are you aware of anything new which may be of interest?'

'I suppose this could be of interest, Sir; I put it to the side of the Board as I don't know if it's connected, but there was a road traffic incident in the small hours of the morning. Circa four a.m., about seven miles from the cottage. Single male, car overturned after taking a bend too fast. He was cut out of the car and taken to hospital in a bad way, still unconscious when I last checked.'

'And what made you think this could be connected?'

'Just, well, the car was heading in a direction away from the cottage on not a widely used road. He was in a rush, and it happened in the early hours of the morning. Oh, and the car had false registration plates.'

I look at her, all eager to make a difference, wanting to find links in everything, just like I and probably others were when we first started out in plain clothes. But it's good, this is the kind of thinking I like.

'How did you get on to this?'

'I contacted the traffic team to see if there are any traffic or speed cameras in the area so that I could trawl through any recordings or photos.'

'And, who put you on that task?'

'Well, er, no one, Sir, I just thought…'

'Umm, I like your initiative, Joanna. Follow it up, will you?'

'Yes, Sir, right away.'

I see her eyes light up. 'And Joanna, it's Boss, not Sir,' with a small smile indicating my appreciation for her good work.

'Er… yes… Boss.'

'Now, I know I shouldn't ask this, but is there any chance of a coffee before I go back into the interview room? I'm in need of some caffeine.'

She looks at me with that confidence of knowing what passes for correct or not these days in the workplace and smiles back at me, 'Not a problem, Boss. I'll get it now.'

12

Martin – Mylesham Police Station

Back in the interview room, the DS restarts the recording device. After considering the situation further, my solicitor has advised me to reply "No comment" to any questions, but I feel that makes me look guilty of something, and I have nothing to hide. She says the police are considering me a prime suspect and that I had the means, the opportunity, and the motive to do this awful thing.

Thinking about it, she has a point. If you look at this logically, the police have me banged to rights for this; it's too easy for them, but I can't let them do that. Admittedly, it does not look good for me right now, and I need Melissa to recover and support me in this.

DI Robbins then breaks the silence, 'Now, Martin, firstly, I remind you that you remain under caution.'

'Yes.'

'Was there any altercation between the four of you in the cottage or with any other person that weekend?'

'No.'

'Do you know of anyone or any reason for someone to hold a grudge or grievance against either your wife or your friend Craig?'

'Do you mean other than the two of them having an affair?' and as soon as I say these words, I realise I've just provided the motive for me to harm them, and they're both looking directly at me. My solicitor touches my arm, we look at each other, and then I turn back to Robbins and add, 'I didn't do this; I didn't know they were having an affair behind my back. Anyway, who said it was an affair? It could have just happened there and then that night, a heat of the moment thing.'

Robbins doesn't reply to my question. He moves on.

'OK, that aside for the moment, what about another person? Is there anyone else that you are aware of that would want to harm either of them?'

Based on that question, he already thinks I have a motive. All I can think about is the threat Craig mentioned yesterday regarding his work. 'Well, yes, but in relation to Craig though, not Tanya. Craig told me he had received a threat from someone, some mobster or gangster or whatever, tied in with a property and development deal in London that had gone wrong involving tens of millions of pounds, and he is...,' I correct myself, 'was leading the legal team on behalf of the Insurance company. The Insurers suspect there is criminal activity involved and are looking for ways not to pay out. Craig was following their instructions, and this person or group was pressuring him to decide in their favour; he was stuck between a rock and a hard place.'

'Craig told you this. When?'

'Yesterday afternoon. He told me the police are investigating the development deal and the verbal threat he received. I jotted down some notes yesterday afternoon in my pocketbook; it'll be beside my bed. I thought it would make a decent plot for a book.'

'A book?'

'Yes, I'm a fiction author; I try to weave my thriller stories around things that can happen in real life.'

The DS speaks, 'Much like this situation we find ourselves in now then.'

I turn my head to him, 'Really? My wife and friend are dead, and you're making light of it?'

'Er no, that's not what I meant, I meant…'

Robbins interrupts him, 'Tell me more about this development deal and threat. You mentioned tens of millions are involved?'

My focus goes back to Robbins. 'Craig said it could be as much as one hundred million pounds, the value of the insurance cover. I presume that is big enough money to be killed over?'

'Some will kill for just a few grand; you'd be surprised. Do you know anything more? Do you have any names?'

'No, not really. He said it was privileged information and shouldn't have told me what he had, but he was concerned and worried. He said the threat was from a senior person in this construction company, a large family-run business. Some of the investment may have come from dodgy proceeds, you know. Craig hinted at organised crime. I don't know the names, but the police are looking into it, and I'm sure you can find out more information from his law firm.'

'Thank you, we'll look into that. We will have logged your notebook into evidence, so we'll look at that also. Is there anyone else you can think of?'

'What? Is that not enough for you?'

'It may be, but we need to be sure there are no other threats, concerns, or leads. What about your wife, Tanya? Does anything come to mind in relation to her?'

'No.' I look at my solicitor, writing notes beside me, and direct my next comment to her. 'This is getting ridiculous.' I look back to Robbins, 'You have me down as the prime suspect, don't you? Well, you're mistaken. I loved my wife, and I loved Craig as a friend. Yes, I'm hurt over this affair thing, but not enough that I'd kill them, for God's sake. Get real.'

'Look, Martin, I respect this is a difficult time for you, and we can appreciate what a trauma this must be. But we must ask difficult questions now to help find the killer. I'm sorry for putting you through this, but yes, we do consider you a suspect at this time for obvious reasons.'

Kaja stops writing and addresses Robbins. 'Are you charging my client, or is he free to go?'

Looking at his wristwatch, he takes the opportunity to flip procedure back on my solicitor, 'We can detain your client for some ten hours yet, and if I so wish, I can seek a further twelve-hour extension. Your client is a suspect, and we need to be clear on the extent of your client's involvement, granted, if any, in these murders. Any charge will come from the CPS if they deem it appropriate based on information we collect.'

I chip in, looking at Kaja. 'Can they?' Her return, with a slow nod, says it all.

Robbins starts again, 'Now Martin, let's go over events once more. What brought you all together this weekend?'

I sit quietly and consider my position, looking at Robbins. I have tried to help, but they see me as the prime suspect. I can feel frustration building, and I could end up saying the wrong thing. It's time I thought about my own situation, my protection.

'Martin?' he asks.

My reply is short, 'No Comment.'

13

Melissa – Mylesham Hospital

Sunday Night, 11th June

Waking up, I feel drained and can recall snippets of some really weird dreams. Opening my eyes, I notice that the room is dimly lit and unrecognisable. Pushing myself up on the bed, a wave of nausea runs through me, and I feel sick. I see the drip in my left hand and then register a low beeping sound to my left; as I turn my head to look at the machine, my head spins, and the nausea wave hits me again. Seeing the disposable sick bowl on the bed beside me, I pick it up, expecting to vomit, but I just gag; there's nothing to come out. My lips and mouth are dry, and I'm thirsty. What the hell happened? Why am I here?

Slowly panning around the room, clearly, I'm in a hospital bed in a small room to myself. To my right is a large glass window overlooking a corridor and a nurse station with two nurses sitting behind the desk.

A nurse looks up and notices me. She picks up a telephone while looking and saying something to the other nurse, who then stands, leaves the desk, and crosses the corridor, heading towards me. She opens the door and enters.

'Hello, Melissa. How do you feel?'

'I feel sick. What am I doing in here?

'You will feel sick for a few hours yet, it's only natural considering what happened. You were admitted early this morning with suspected alcohol poisoning. You've responded well to treatment, rehydration, and monitoring, and we expect you'll be up and about in the next day or so; probably feeling a little rough, though. We don't anticipate there being any long-lasting damage or effects.'

'Where's my husband, Craig? Is he OK?'

'He's not here, I'm afraid.'

'Can I call him then? I want him here.'

'Er, no, that won't be possible, Melissa. Now let's just check your BP and oxygen levels.'

That's a funny response. 'Why can't I phone him?' She doesn't respond; she just carries on noting the readings down on a clipboard. 'Why can't I call him? What's going on here?'

She stops writing and looks at me quite seriously, which unnerves me. 'The Doctor will be here any second. He'll let you know what has happened.'

'What do you mean *what has happened*? I want to speak with Craig now,' my voice rising and forceful, and by her reaction, it startles the young nurse. The door opens again, and a doctor, accompanied by the other nurse, enters, approaching the bedside with his hands elevated slightly as though he is trying to calm me down. 'Where is my husband?'

The Doctor speaks first, 'Mrs Tyler, Melissa. Please try to remain calm. You've been through quite an event, and you need to give yourself some time to recover.'

Focusing straight on the Doctor, in a raised voice, I launch at him, 'Why won't you tell me what is going on? Where is my husband?' and as I do, my head pounds, and I grimace.

The Doctor turns to the nurse and says something that I couldn't make out.

'Yes, Doctor,' and she leaves the room. He then looks back at me.

'Melissa, we have something to tell you about your husband, but I need you to remain calm. Can you do that for me, please?'

'Cut the crap, what's happened to Craig?'

'Melissa, your husband is dead; he passed away last night.'

I look at him, not moving, not breathing. Craig is dead; is this another weird dream? He looks at me with concern across his face; he's serious. 'What do you mean he's dead? How can he be dead? We're on holiday, a weekend break from work; he can't be dead; we were just having a party in the cottage.'

The Doctor continues, not averting his eyes from me, 'The police want to speak with you about what happened.'

'The police? Why? Was there an accident? Craig can't be dead; you must have the wrong person; there's been a mistake.'

'No, I'm sorry, Melissa, there is no mistake. Your husband, Craig, and, I understand, your friend, Tanya, are both dead, and the police are treating their deaths as suspicious.'

As I look at him, trying to comprehend what he's saying, our eyes fix on each other; I only half notice the nurse return and begin injecting something into the cannula in the back of my hand. I start to feel lightheaded, and as I speak, my eyes are closing, 'What happened to…'

Just as my eyes close again, I hear one of the nurses say, 'Poor thing, her husband and her friend,' and a distant reply, 'I know, it's just terrible.'

14

DI Robbins – Mylesham Police Station

Monday Morning, 12th June

Everyone wants a fast result on this, and the CPS have just confirmed they are happy to charge Martin Nicholson on two counts of murder. It's obvious the Chief Constable wants to be on the news again, showing the public how quickly West Ryshire Constabulary arrests and charges criminals on his watch. But it's all a bit too fast for me; there is this driver in hospital that may be connected; he may be the killer, and Nicholson could be completely innocent.

We need to I.D. this driver and check for any evidence of him being in the cottage, in that bedroom, and we'll need a motive. Hansen thinks the driver is involved somehow, but Colin disagrees, arguing it's just a coincidence. Hansen is saying his motive could be as simple as a burglary gone wrong, or a warped fantasy to kill with a sword, or some other motive yet to be established. But Martin Nicholson fulfils all three criteria right now for sure; there is not much more we need to prove if anything, but my instincts are telling me it's all a bit too neatly tied up if we nail our colours on Martin; we should keep in mind other potential offenders. But the clock is ticking.

Standing from my desk, I walk to my office door. I lean on the door frame, pushing my head through into the wider office. Looking over at Hansen, I call out, 'DC Hansen, my office, please. I want an update on the car and the driver.'

'Yes, Boss,' she calls out, standing up from behind her computer screen.

Within a minute, Hansen is in my office, standing by my desk with a bundle of papers and polythene bags held in her left arm; I'm straight to the point.

'OK, so what do we have on the driver and the car?'

'Still no I.D. at the moment, Boss, nothing on him to indicate who he is. We've taken his prints at the hospital and await feedback to see if he's on the system. We're hoping for a match, but it may take some time as his hands are cut up badly and swollen, possibly trying to get out of the car or protect himself as it rolled.'

'What about a photo likeness, facial recognition?'

'No, same problem, smashed up, bruised, swollen; it'll be some time before he looks like he used to if he's lucky. His own mother wouldn't recognise him in that state.'

I sigh, 'OK, so what about the car?'

'The VIN shows the registered owner living in Sheffield. It was stolen a few days ago from a shopping centre there. Our man had changed the registration plates for false ones, using an identical car but a different owner. We've checked; he's cloned their car.'

'Sounds planned. So then, piece it together for me; what do we know?'

'At around four a.m., about seven miles from the murder scene at the cottage, the car spins off the road, hits a dry-stone wall, flips and rolls over a few times, ending up upside down in a ditch.' Hansen places a couple of A4 size colour photos of the car and scene in front of me. 'Looks like he was the only occupant. The local uniform checked around to make sure there was no one else injured who crawled away. According to the

Traffic Incident Officer, he was travelling way too fast for the road and lost it on the narrow bend near the farmhouse. Noise of the crash woke the Farmer and his wife, and she called it in whilst he went out to help, although there was not much he could do when he got there other than keep the driver's head up out of the ditch water, otherwise he probably would have drowned. Fire Service had to cut him out of the car, and he was taken to hospital in a bad way in the Air Ambulance; he was still unconscious the last time I checked. Fire crew at the scene said he wasn't wearing a seatbelt, which accounts for the extensive injuries. We have uniform with him, waiting for him to come around; well, assuming he does, I should say. It looks like he wanted to get away from somewhere fast.'

Lifting the photos and passing them back to Hansen, 'Or going somewhere fast. He's that bad, eh?'

'Yes, Boss, he's pretty mashed up.'

'Right, so is there any connection with the cottage and this double murder?'

'Yes, I think there is. While waiting for the emergency crews to arrive on the scene, the Farmer said the driver kept slipping in and out of consciousness, and the Farmer tried his best to keep him awake. The driver wasn't making any sense, mumbling, and moaning a lot, but the Farmer's Wife said she thought he mumbled "*dead, both of them*" a couple of times, although the Farmer doesn't agree with her. As the paramedics were treating him at the scene before airlifting him to the hospital, officers searched his pockets for I.D. and didn't find any, nor did they find a mobile phone, which these days is a little unusual. But they did find this,' passing me a clear polythene evidence bag containing a small scrap of paper containing some handwritten words, she continues, 'it is water damaged, but you can just make out it's the address of the cottage. Officers on the scene didn't think anything of it, but when they returned to the station and informed the Sergeant of this and of what the Farmer's Wife had thought she heard, he thought it prudent to visit the cottage and check it out; at worst, he thought it might help identify the driver. So, they went to the cottage and found our victims and the other two; that's how all this came about. We've tested the paper for prints, but nothing of any use.'

'Right. Well, we need to find out more about this guy and how he fits in with events, if at all. It could still be unrelated; Colin could be right, it could be a coincidence; he could be an unregistered worker who did some work on the property for cash, or someone in the pub said, "*Here's a nice holiday cottage*" but it feels unlikely, especially with the stolen car element. Make sure we get a DNA sample from the driver and have it processed quickly; put some pressure on the lab guys.' I hand the evidence bag back to Hansen.

'Yes, Boss.'

'Good work, keep it up, Joanna.'

'Thanks, Boss.'

She leaves my office, directing her mobile phone to her ear as she walks away. So, we have one suspect, the husband, clearly at the scene, prints on the murder weapon, and he has a very clear motive. Then we have this guy, speeding away from the scene, at or about the right time frame of the murders, with the cottage address found in his pocket, in a stolen car with false plates, professionally cloned. I'm confident we have our man, but I'm not sure which one of them it is, they could even have been working together. For the time being, all I can do is keep the heat on the husband as the time limit to detain him is about to run out.

15

Melissa – Mylesham Hospital

Late Monday Morning, 12th June

Whatever the nurse injected me with last night knocked me out again, and I slept right through until a nightmare woke me just after nine-thirty a.m. The nurse came to check my blood pressure and oxygen levels again, and she informed me that the police were expected to arrive at about eleven a.m. to interview me; in about ten minutes now. I still don't have any further information other than Craig and Tanya are both dead, and the police are questioning a man as their deaths are suspicious.

There was a brief mention of the incident during the breakfast news on the television, but there were no further facts or details, just that there had been a double murder, a man is helping the police with their inquiries, and one female remains in hospital; that'll be me I suppose. So, is this man Martin then? Is he a suspect, or is he really helping them, trying to find the person who killed Craig and Tanya?

This is bad, though; it's really bad. I can't tell the police what I know, or I could become a suspect. I shouldn't have done it; it was a stupid thing to do, but I never thought it would end up like this.

Dad is on his way to sit with me when the police arrive; I was hoping he would have been here by now. I'm terrified of being interviewed by detectives from the Major Crime Unit. They could trip me up and make me say something I don't want to. Come on, Dad, where are you?

The nurse opens the door and brings in a fresh jug of water and a couple of clean glasses, placing them on the small cupboard beside my bed.

'Is my dad back yet? Have you seen him?'

'No, not yet. I'm sure he'll be here any minute. He's probably stuck in the road works just down the road. Are you OK, Melissa?'

'No, not really. I'm not looking forward to this interview. I want to know more about what happened, but then again, I don't. Does that sound crazy?'

'Not at all; I know what you mean, but at least they will provide you with more information about what happened and who this man is they are questioning.'

'I think I know who it is, but I'm hoping I'm wrong.'

'Oh, who?'

'My friend's husband; he was with us at the cottage, and he's not been to see me, and no one has said he's missing or in hospital or anything yet, really.'

'That is strange, I suppose. So, he could be the man they are talking to?'

'Yes, I suppose so.'

The knock at the door announces the arrival of two strangers to my room, and we both look at them standing in the doorway.

The man speaks, 'Good morning. Mrs Melissa Tyler?'

'Yes,' I reply as the nurse adjusts the sheets on my bed.

'May we come in? I believe you have been expecting us; I'm Detective Inspector Paul Robbins, of the Mylesham Major Crime Unit, and this is my colleague, Detective Constable Joanna Hansen.'

'Yes, of course,' my reply, now worried my dad isn't here yet. They enter, pull up two chairs, and sit beside the bed. The Detective Constable opens a folio, places it on her knees, and extracts a pen from her jacket pocket. DI Robbins begins.

'Firstly, we are very sorry for the loss of your husband, Craig, and your close friend, Tanya Nicholson. My DC here will take some notes of this conversation so that we can piece together what happened over the weekend. You are not under caution; you are simply assisting us with our enquiries; is that OK, Mrs Tyler?'

'Er, yes. My father is on his way here, and I want him to sit with me through this if you don't mind?'

'Of course, but we do need to move along quickly for obvious reasons; will he be long?'

'No, he said he would be here when you arrived; he's not normally late when he says he'll be somewhere.'

'Well, if we can just run through some formalities first, that will be useful; is that OK?'

'Yes, I suppose so.'

After tidying the bed sheets, the nurse advises she will step outside, but I should press the call button if needed.

DC Hansen then speaks up, 'Can you please confirm your full name and home address?'

'Yes, Melissa Emily Tyler, 37 Hamilton Road, Green Park, York.'

'And your husband's full name?'

'Craig Tyler.'

'He lived at the same address?'

That throws me a little, her use of "*lived at*". She looks up from her pad at my pause and realises her choice of words. 'I'm sorry, Mrs Tyler.'

'He is dead then?'

'Yes, I'm afraid so. His body has been formally identified by his brother.'

Tears start to well up, and inside, I want to scream out; I can't think of what to say in reply. Robbins sees this, and I suppose it's his experience that steps in.

'Would you like some water, Mrs Tyler?'

I phase out for a few moments, my mind escaping the situation, the reality of what has happened and is happening.

'Mrs Tyler?'

I sniff and dab my eyes with a tissue. 'No. No, thank you. And Tanya, she is dead also?'

'Yes.' He continues, 'We need you to tell us what happened on Saturday evening into Sunday morning last weekend, Mrs Tyler. We are piecing together statements and events to get a clear picture of what occurred. If you don't mind, can you describe what happened after you returned from the pub following dinner on Saturday evening?'

'Yes, I'll try.' I sigh, take another deep breath, hold it, and then release it, trying to steady myself before starting. I notice my voice is shaky, and my hands are trembling slightly. 'We walked back in the dark on Saturday night, cutting across the fields. We had all been drinking, so we left the cars at the cottage. We got back, Martin went straight in and lit the log burner, Tanya and I prepared some snacks, and Craig stayed outside for a few minutes, looking up at the stars. I went out to Craig with a couple of glasses of wine, and we chatted for a few minutes before going inside. Nothing unusual, I suppose. We were all drinking wine, there was some music on, we laughed, danced a bit, ate some cheese; we were just having a good time. I started to get very sleepy, the air, food, and wine, I suppose; although I don't recall making my way up to bed, I do recall looking at the bedside clock, which said eleven-thirty-three, yes, eleven-thirty-three.'

'And Craig, Tanya and Martin remained downstairs; is that correct?' he asks.

'Yes, I presume so. Although one of them must have helped me upstairs, I can't remember who or much of anything else after getting into bed, save for looking at the clock; I must have gone to sleep more or less straight away.'

'How much wine do you think you consumed?' he asks me.

'All of us or me personally?'

'You, personally.'

'I don't know; we had a couple of bottles of wine with dinner, some earlier in the day, then I suppose, I don't know, at least another couple of bottles back at the cottage. Maybe I had about six or eight large glasses, maybe a little more, but I wasn't counting. Why?'

'On the Sunday morning, police officers attending the cottage were unable to wake you, and you were rushed in here; the Emergency Team said it was alcohol poisoning. So, you must have consumed a lot, I suppose, possibly more than that? Would you say you did?'

'I don't know, I wouldn't think it was any more than we normally drink when we get together. The empty bottles will be lined up in the utility room; Craig often stacks all our empties so we can be ashamed of ourselves when checking out. You know, for a laugh.' The thought of Craig doing this brings tears to my eyes; I can't hold them in, and I start to cry.

As DI Robbins was passing me another tissue, the door opens, and my dad rushes in, straight on the offensive. 'What the hell are you doing? Can't you see my daughter is in no fit state to be interviewed by the police? You should be ashamed of yourselves.'

DC Hansen stands to square up to Dad, dropping some of her papers on the floor. DI Robbins quickly grabs her forearm firmly and nods for her to sit back down again. Dad walks around the bed and wraps his arms around me, one of the protective embraces only a father can provide. I nuzzle into his chest and hear his muffled words, 'Unbelievable. What, could you not wait until I got here?'

Robbins replies, 'And you are, Mister?'

'Parker. Melissa's father. And you two are?'

'DI Robbins and DC Hansen, Major Crime Unit.'

Dad doesn't say anything further; he just holds me. The silence in the room is deafening; one of them will need to break the deadlock, but nobody seems to want to. I suppose DC Hansen won't, and DI Robbins has experience in knowing how to diffuse a situation rather than ignite one. The attention is on me; I can feel the charged atmosphere, and I need to be the one to break this. Still in Dad's embrace, I muffle out the words, 'How did Craig and Tanya die?'

DI Robbins coughs slightly in his throat, regaining formalities, 'They were murdered; they died at the same time.'

Breaking from Dad's arms, I move back against the pillows propped on the steel bed frame. Dad takes a deep breath and slowly releases it, pulling in a chair from the corner of the room.

'I think I know that bit, Inspector; I know they're dead, but *how* did they die?'

I notice DC Hansen looking up at her superior while he remains looking at me. Dad takes hold of my right hand and squeezes it tightly.

'They were killed at the same time, with a sword in the downstairs bedroom.'

Oh my god, he said a sword. A sword! I squeeze Dad's hand tighter, and he puts his left hand on my upper arm, showing support; he is here for me. I don't know what to say to this; killed with a sword, what like chopped up, sliced, heads removed. I start to shake visibly.

'I'm sorry, Mrs Tyler, you would have found out soon; this is the kind of murder that the press gets very interested in.'

I look at the Inspector through tear-filled eyes, 'Who did this? Do you think it was Martin? Why would he? No, not Martin; he wouldn't have done that. Why would someone take them into the spare bedroom to kill them but leave us alone upstairs, sleeping?'

These questions land heavily on the Detective Inspector; he looks lost for words. Hansen takes the opportunity to chip in, 'Good questions that we are looking for answers to. Did you notice anyone suspicious around the cottage, nearby in the woods, anyone that looked out of place?'

Turning my head to her, 'No, not that I can recall. There was no issue in the village or pub either; everything was fine. From what I can remember, they were all very jolly when I went to bed. No, it wasn't Martin. I can't accept that. Why do you think he could have done it?'

Robbins, recomposed, answers, 'Because they died in each other's arms, in the act of lovemaking. Craig was lying on top of Tanya, and the sword was pushed through them both. They were having an illicit affair, and Martin's fingerprints are on the sword.'

I look at Dad; we are both slowly shaking our heads from side to side in disbelief.

Robbins continues, 'That would explain why you and Martin were not also killed; you were upstairs asleep, out of it, an innocent party, and Martin was the offender.'

Throwing myself at Dad, he embraces me again, and I start to cry profusely, almost hysterically. Both police officers stand, mumbling something I cannot hear, and they leave the room.

16

DC Joanna Hansen – Mylesham Police Station

Monday Afternoon, 12th June

Reading through a copy of Melissa Tyler's interview transcript from this morning, she said, *"I wouldn't think it was any more than we normally drink when we get together"*, and it rings a little alarm bell with me, somewhere Martin said something similar, now where is it? I open a scanned copy of the notes the attending Sergeant took when he arrived at the cottage, and he noted, *"MN - I don't recall drinking that much"*. That's an interesting coincidence; they both said similar things without knowing the other had said it, but then the Sergeant noted that MN *"seemed to be still under the influence of alcohol"* when they arrived at the cottage yesterday morning, with Melissa ending up in hospital with alcohol poisoning; that's strange. They both went to bed before the two victims, so their intake stopped then.

So, where did this extra alcohol come from?

Turning to the computer screen again, I tap in the case reference and search for the hospital report on Melissa. It's there but hasn't been opened and reviewed; there is no comment on it, nothing. I click on the file, and the medical report opens on the screen. Reading the A&E comments and diagnosis of alcohol poisoning, the treatment comprised rehydration with intravenous fluids, oxygen, and bed rest with monitoring observations, and all seems in order. There is also a note about blood samples being taken for testing over concern about possible organ damage, but the results are not attached. I continue the search for the blood results but can't find them, so decide to call the hospital directly, and eventually, I'm put through to the ward that Melissa is on.

'Good afternoon. I'm Detective Constable Joanna Hansen. I'm calling about Melissa Tyler, a patient on your ward, I believe.'

'Yes, she is, that's correct. How can I help you, Detective?'

'I am reading through a copy of the medical notes sent to us earlier today and note that blood tests were requested in A&E yesterday before Melissa was admitted to the ward. Do you have a copy of the blood test results to hand?'

'One moment, let me just see what we have on the system… sorry, bear with me; it's not the quickest of systems… should I call you back, Detective?'

'No, it's OK. I'll wait. Is that alright?'

'Yes, one moment.'

I can hear faint keyboard tapping from the nurse as I scroll file notes on my computer, typing in search words for alcohol and test results, but nothing new appears. After a few minutes, a voice comes over the phone, 'Ah yes, here we go. Yes, I have the results.'

'Good. Was there anything unusual found in Melissa's blood?'

'What, besides the alcohol levels?'

'Yes.'

'Well, yes, there are noted high levels of a benzodiazepine related medication, quite high actually. Was this a suicide attempt, Detective? She was lucky to be found in time.'

'What does benzodiazepine do?'

'Typically, it's used as sleep medication; from this, I would suggest this is likely to be prescribed sleeping pills.'

So that's how the two of them survived the night; either another person entered the cottage and didn't know they were both upstairs but unconscious, or Martin Nicholson tried to poison Melissa, but he didn't take as much so he wouldn't die from it, making him look like a victim as well. In the latter, he could have drugged Melissa, then went to bed himself, then come back downstairs and killed them both before taking some of the medication himself. I need to see if Martin had the same drug in his blood and, if so, how much.

'Ah, OK. Thank you. Please can you email a copy of that report to me?'

'Yes, of course; what is your email address, Detective?'

After hanging up, I mull over this information; it wasn't just alcohol that affected Melissa; it could have been Martin who did this, or it could have been Craig and Tanya so that their respective partners would be asleep and none the wiser whilst they carried on downstairs. If it's the latter, I need to know how it was administered to Melissa and Martin without them knowing.

Looking through the evidence log and scene photos, I note the empty wine bottles in the kitchen area: two white and two red. Flicking through the CSI records, the wine bottles have been retained as evidence, so I pick up the phone to the lab to see if any tests have been carried out.

17

DI Robbins – Mylesham Police Station

Monday Evening, 12th June

I'm not one hundred percent convinced of this, but I have my instructions from above; at seven twenty-five this evening, Martin Nicholson was formally charged with the murder of his wife, Tanya Nicholson, the murder of his friend, Craig Tyler and the attempted murder of his friend's wife, Melissa Tyler. I can understand the first two, for those don't look good for him, but the last charge doesn't really make any sense; if he wanted Melissa dead, she would be as he had all the time in the world to kill her while she slept. But then, why kill them and then just go back to bed? It doesn't make sense. I tried to get a further extension to hold him before charging him, up to the maximum ninety-six hours, but was told to stop wasting time and to "*just get on with it*". It didn't help his case when lower levels of the sleeping medication were found in his blood results, and the drug used was the same as he had been prescribed last year when being treated for depression.

When we read the charges to him in the Custody Suite, he nearly collapsed, his knees buckled, with Colin catching him before he hit the floor. There was no real protest from his solicitor, Miss Wójcik; I suppose she can see how it all looks, although she did make a good point that the sleeping pills may have been administered by Craig or Tanya so that they could spend some uninterrupted time together and thus, another person could be involved.

I still think there are some open questions relating to that driver, but as he's in no fit state to be interviewed, let alone whether he's going to live, the decision has been made to push ahead with charging Martin Nicholson. Granted, the only two things pointing to the driver are a scrap of paper with the cottage address on it and the possible misheard words by the farmer's wife. It's a big mistake in my opinion to rule out the driver at this stage and focus on Nicholson, but my opinion doesn't seem to count for a great deal in the higher halls of law enforcement; *what happened to due process?*

My boss also wanted to wait to see where this other line of enquiry would go, but no, he is under the same instructions as me from up on high to push ahead with Nicholson.

Given the charges of murder, I fully expected Martin Nicholson to be held in custody until his court hearing, but maybe because I, supported by my DCI, have put up a plausible argument in relation to a second line of enquiry, it was agreed that Martin could be released under investigation. Whilst I didn't agree with charging him so quickly, at least he is not being held on remand.

I've decided to leave young Hansen on the driver; she is keen and bright, and I like her passion for the job; we need his identity to see if there are any links to all of this, and she'll get it, and she'll find out who he is. We also need to get a proper formal statement out of Melissa Tyler.

Picking up the phone, I type in Colin's extension, and he picks up immediately. 'Colin, can you check on Melissa Tyler at the hospital and arrange a time to visit her again tomorrow afternoon? I have to be in court in the morning on another matter.'

'Yes, Boss, not a problem; is it me with you, or are you taking young Hansen again?'

'You; I've put Hansen onto the driver and want her focussed on that while we get to the bottom of what actually happened in that cottage.'

'No probs, Boss. I'll get on it straight away.'

18

Melissa Tyler – Mylesham Hospital

Early Tuesday Afternoon, 13th June

Dad is here with me this time, waiting for the police to arrive. The hospital has discharged me, and I'm packed, ready to leave and head for home; well, back to Mum and Dad's place. I don't think I can face going back home to our house just yet with Craig gone.

'It'll be OK, love. Just tell them what you know, and then we can get out of here.'

'I already have; there is nothing new to add that I can think of.'

'Then just tell them that, and we'll be off.'

I have wanted to talk with someone about this, but it's been difficult while I've been in here. This is my first real opportunity to discuss things. 'Dad, do you think Martin could have done this?'

'Not the Martin I know, no. But the police do see him as a prime suspect, and well, he was there. Who else would want to ki… do what they did?'

'Craig did seem a bit weird a few weeks back; he mentioned something about being extra careful, to be more aware of strangers. I just thought it was his new job; maybe there is someone out there that wanted to harm him.'

'You should mention this to the police,' and as Dad says these words, there is a knock at the door announcing the arrival of the police.

It's DI Robbins again but with a different colleague this time. 'Good morning, Mrs Tyler,' then looking at Dad, 'Sir,' slightly nodding his head, 'Is it OK if we come in?'

'Yes, we've been expecting you,' Dad replies.

They pull up some chairs, and DI Robbins introduces his colleague DS Paul Holt, who proceeds to take out a notebook, flip it open and poise with pen in hand.

'Firstly, Mrs Tyler, I have to inform you we have charged a person with the murders of your husband and your friend.'

'You have? Who is it?' Dad interjects before I can say anything. DI Robbins looks at Dad, then turns to look at me as he answers.

'Mr Martin Nicholson.'

'Really? He did this?'

'Well, he has been charged with the offences; the decision will come from a jury.'

Dad again asks on my behalf, 'So he has been charged with double murder?'

'Yes, and one count of attempted murder.'

'Who did he attempt to murder?' beating Dad to it this time.

'You, Melissa.'

'No. No one attempted to kill me; I now remember going to bed, climbing upstairs, well, crawling really, using my hands on the stairs. I can recall that now, and I remember Craig went with me, and that's where you found me the following morning; I just drank too much and went to bed. I don't see how Martin could have done this. I'm sorry. It's not him.'

'When you were first admitted to hospital, the medical team thought it was alcohol poisoning and took some blood samples to be sure and to check there was no other organ damage. Yes, there was a high alcohol content in your blood, but something else was detected, and after further testing, it seems that the white wine was spiked with crushed sleeping pills. We believe Martin Nicholson tried to overdose you to kill you as well.'

'Oh my god; that can't be true.'

Dad chips in, 'Mel, tell them what you told me earlier; tell them about Craig and…'

DI Robbins looks at me, 'Have you remembered something that may be of interest?'

'Yes, possibly. Recently, Craig was made a Partner with his law firm and a few weeks ago, and he mentioned I should be a little more vigilant, keep an eye out for strangers, and be more alert. When I questioned why, he kind of brushed it off, saying all new Partners are advised of this.' After finishing saying this, they look at each other and then back at me. DI Robbins comments as DS Holt scribbles down some notes.

'That is a little unusual. I don't think either of us has come across that kind of briefing advice to new Partners. We can ask his law firm partners about it, though. Was there something in particular that concerned him?'

'No, not that I'm aware of; he never mentioned it again.'

'Did Craig seem distracted or troubled by anything?'

'Yes, all the time. He always invested his time heavily in cases; even when he was not at work, he was really. It was hard at times, as it felt like he wasn't even in the room with me when he was sitting opposite me. He was often on his phone with email and text messages at all times of day and night; does that make sense?'

'Umm, yes, I suppose it does. Thank you. Is there anything else you can remember?'

I look at Dad, then back to the Detective, 'The last time we spoke, you mentioned they were both killed with a sword.'

'Yes, that is correct.'

'And you said Martin's fingerprints were on the sword that killed them?'

'Yes.'

'Can you tell me if the sword was one of those from the wall in the living room? Because if it was, both Martin and Craig were playing around with it on Saturday afternoon. That would explain Martin's prints on the sword, wouldn't it?'

'Yes… I suppose it would.'

'Well, then it could be someone else who picked up the sword to kill them, couldn't it?'

He pauses before he replies, stalling a little, like he's trying to decide how to answer my question.

'Conceivably, yes, it could.'

19

DC Hansen – Mylesham Police Station

Late Morning, Wednesday 14th June

Each avenue I take to identify this driver comes up blank. There is no missing person report that fits his description, although, in his current physical condition, it would be easy to misinterpret his description; he had no I.D. on him, and nothing was found in or about the stolen car, save for the address of the cottage. Our only hope is that he either wakes up and tells us his identity or he has a past criminal record from a run-in with the police, and his DNA is contained on the national DNA database, matching an earlier stored sample. I chased the testing lab first thing this morning, but they still didn't have the result to compare against the database; they expect to provide a result sometime today.

Waiting for news, I review all the information I have about the car, the road it was on, the route it would have taken if it had come from the cottage, the emergency teams that attended, the statements from the Farmer and his wife, and the attending police officers.

I tip back in my chair and close my eyes. Who are you? What were you doing? If you killed them, why?

The gods above believe they have their man, Nicholson. He was charged on Monday, but I'm not sure. Yes, it could be him, but is it? This driver is frustrating the hell out of me. It could be him working alone or with Nicholson. The patio door was open, so he would have had easy access. He was driving fast away from the scene at speed. The DS thinks it's circumstantial at best, but I'm not sure. His reason for being on that lane at that time in the morning in a stolen car needs resolving.

I continue flicking through the evidence log, desperately looking for a link to the cottage other than the address on a piece of paper, when, "Ping", an email lands in my Inbox from the Traffic Police that attended the crash scene that morning. I click it open and start reading it through. Traffic recovered the car from the ditch and took it down to Swimpton Yard for technical inspection. Over the last day or so, they have been running all the usual checks on brakes, steering, and tyres and found they were operating normally, or at least from what was left, they can say that. They conducted a fingertip search of the car and contents and found a broken mobile phone, a cheap burner type, wedged between the passenger seat and seat upright. It was bagged and registered in the evidence log for the traffic incident, not the murder evidence log. The phone was then passed to the local tech guys, and they managed to recover the memory card from inside. Upon opening, they found the attached.

I look at the top of the email again and see the attached image file. Double-clicking the file opens it, and I click the expand button to fill my screen. Unbelievable. "Sarge!" I shout out, but to no reply. Standing, I look around but can't see him; there are only a couple of other people in the room with headphones on. This is hot information I've got to get to the Boss, and I start to dial his mobile number when another email lands in my Inbox; it's from the Bio testing lab, the driver's DNA results. I place my mobile down on the desktop and sit down again. Moving the cursor across to the new email, I'm willing this to be good news; come on, come on, and open the email. 'YES!' we have a match.

One Dimitri Hatzis. I tap his name into the computer and get an instant hit in the police database. He is linked to a number of allegations involving intimidation and extortion, with suspected links to organised crime groups in the south of England. His DNA is on the database after he was caught up in a raid that failed to bag any senior players, and he went down for four years in September 2014, refusing to turn on the crime group.

Wow! This supports what Martin Nicholson said about Craig being threatened and Melissa's comment in her statement. The Boss will want to know these two golden nuggets of information right away, so I pick up my mobile again and dial him. As it rings, I start to think the DS is going to be annoyed with me; he said there was nothing in this line of enquiry, and as I listen to the phone ring tone, a wild idea crosses my mind: *the DS is not involved, is he?* No, don't be silly; he just honestly believed there was no link, repeating my personal mantra, "*Stick to the facts, Jo,*" I wait for the Boss to answer.

'Hi Boss, it's DC Hansen. We have the driver's identity, and we have proof he was in the murder room.'

20

Dimitri – Mylesham Hospital

Evening, Thursday 15th June

The two police detectives enter the private room and sit beside the bed that I'm now handcuffed to. As the door slowly closes, I clock the armed officer standing just outside with my unbandaged right eye. My solicitor remained with me while we waited for the big guns to arrive. He has advised me to reply 'No comment' as though I needed that advice; it's not my first time doing this.

The younger copper pulls out a telescopic, three-legged camera tripod and erects it at the foot on the bed, fixes a small video recorder to the tripod and presses a button on the camera. He then places a portable recording machine on the cupboard beside the bed and plugs the power lead into the wall socket. He presses a button, and the machine emits a high note for what seems a long time before silence returns to the room. The older copper, a DI Robbins, speaks first, confirming his name and rank, followed by DS Holt and reciting those infamous words, putting me under caution.

'This is the first formal interview with Dimitri Hatzis, the time is nineteen forty-six, on Thursday, the fifteenth of June. This interview is in relation to the incident at Fell View Cottage, just outside Bramblehurst Village, on the night of Saturday, the tenth of June. Please state your full name for the recording.'

'Dimitri Paola Hatzis.'

'Mr Hatzis is represented by his solicitor …'

'George Holland.'

'Thank you.' The Inspector continues, 'Now Dimitri, we have been checking through a few things, and we remain a little confused by your earlier revelation to my colleagues. You have admitted to being in the room where Mr Craig Tyler and Mrs Tanya Nicholson were found brutally murdered, but you insist they were already dead before you entered the room. Are you maintaining this position?'

Before I could respond, my solicitor chips in, 'Anything Mr Hatzis said earlier today is not admissible; he was under the influence of medication, and he was not under police caution.'

'Well, thank you, Mr. Holland, for clarifying that point. However, the question still stands: Dimitri, would you like to confirm your earlier comments?'

'No comment.'

'Oh, come on, Dimitri, do you take us for fools?'

'I would like to comment to that, but, taking counsel's advice, it'll have to be no comment.' I smile slightly, giving some pain to the stitched wound on my face.

'OK, Dimitri. Who paid you to kill them?'

'No comment.'

'The Costas family?'

'No comment.'

'All because Craig Tyler wouldn't play ball on the insurance claim?'

'No comment.'

'You're not helping yourself here, Dimitri. You are going down for double murder if you remain at no comment. At least defend yourself, protect yourself. Why take the rap for those who gave you the order?'

'No comment.'

'You have already admitted that you were in the bedroom, and forensics can place you in the room. You even had a photograph on your mobile phone of the two murder victims in that bedroom, photographed after you had killed them, a trophy photo maybe or proof for the boss? You have prior form for violence and intimidation. The Costas family have a motive to make an example out of Craig Tyler, and you carried out their instructions, just like the good foot soldier you are. If you admit to that, we will ask for it to be considered in mitigation during your sentencing.'

'No comment.'

'I never had you down as a murderer, especially of an innocent woman.'

'I didn't kill them.'

My solicitor, Holland, chips in, placing his hand on my handcuffed arm. 'May I remind my client to respond with *no comment*?'

I know that is what I am supposed to say, but they have me banged to rights on this and my ties with the Costas family. I need to think fast here, or I'm getting a double murder rap pinned on me. 'Thank you, I know, but I didn't do this, I swear,' looking at my solicitor.

'Ah, and we are just expected to believe you, is that right, Dimitri? Take your word for it?' Robbins says across the bed at me, hoping I'll bite.

'Yes. I did not do this. They were already dead when I arrived.'

'Really? That's your defence?' Robbins replies.

My solicitor speaks up again, 'Please, gentlemen, my client is recovering from a very serious accident in which he sustained a potentially life-changing head injury along with other significant injuries. This questioning is putting my client under undue stress and strain, putting his recovery at risk. We're calling a halt to this now, thank you.'

'Thank you, Mr Holland. I think you'll find it is I or the senior doctor who will stop this interview, not you, for convenience's sake.' He looks back at me, 'Now Dimitri, what is it to be?'

'No comment.'

'We know about the threat made to Mr Tyler, a threat he considered serious enough to confide in others, which was and is being investigated by the Organised Crime Unit. This doesn't look good for you, does it, Dimitri?'

'No comment.'

'Why use a sword? Now that is old school. What was the message you were trying to send?'

'No comment.'

'Do you have anything further to say?'

'No comment.'

'We found your phone and what was on it. Our tech team is trawling its content, which will lead back to the Costas,' he says, pausing for effect. I know this style of questioning.

'OK, if you have nothing further to add to help yourself, then I suppose you leave me no choice.'

I know what's coming next.

'Dimitri Paola Hatzis, I am arresting you for the murder of Craig Tyler and Tanya Nicholson on the night of the tenth to eleventh of June, contrary to common law. You do not have to say anything. But it may harm your defence if you do not mention when questioned something which you later rely on in court. Anything you do say may be given in evidence. You will remain in police custody. Do you understand?'

'Yes.'

Robbins turns to Holland, directing his next words to my solicitor, 'Now this interview is concluded. The time is… nineteen fifty-three.'

The coppers collect their things together and, without another word, leave the room. I turn my head slowly to look at my solicitor, 'Well, I'm screwed now, aren't I?'

'Only if you did this thing. Look, I'll leave you to get some rest; do not speak with anyone. I'll be back early tomorrow morning, and we'll discuss this further.'

'Yeh, go on. Leave me here chained to this bloody bed. It's not like I'm going anywhere fast, especially with that armed guard out there.'

'Apparently, the guard is for your protection. The police are concerned that someone may visit you to prevent you from talking.'

'What? Come here to bump me off? To stop me talking about what? Watch my lips; I didn't do this.'

'I believe you. Try to get some rest, and I'll see you in the morning.'

21

Martin – Mylesham Police Station

Mid-Morning, Friday 16 June

Well, I'm back here for more questioning, no doubt. My solicitor said it could be like this for the next week or so, and then it could go quiet for a bit.

Kaja comes back into the interview room and asks the police officer to leave us. He sniffs and turns on his heels, leaving the room and closes the door behind him quite firmly, as though he is trying to send a message to me or her. She pulls up a chair alongside mine and leans in close.

Quietly, Kaja speaks, 'I heard late yesterday that the police have a new suspect, one who is getting them excited, if that's the right word to use.'

This jolts me, and I sit upright. 'They have? Who is it?'

'They won't give me his name just yet, but they have confided in me that he is their new prime suspect. Apparently, he was cut free from a crashed car in the early hours of the morning following… you know… about seven miles from the cottage, after taking a bend too quickly, his car clipped a stone wall and overturned into a ditch. He was cut out of the mangled car and taken to hospital with some serious injuries.'

'So how does that make him a suspect?'

'He was sedated for the first few days due to concern over his head injury and possible swelling on the brain, but he regained consciousness early yesterday morning, mumbling incoherently at first, but by late yesterday, the doctors allowed him to be interviewed briefly by the police.'

'And? That still doesn't make him a suspect, does it? What, because he crashed his car into a ditch a few miles away during the early hours of the morning of the night they were killed?'

Kaja sits upright and pulls away from me slightly, probably feeling my hostility to this whole situation, like a volcano with pressure building.

'You seem like you do not want him to be the murderer; is that right?' her accent is seemingly slightly more pronounced, which may be for effect.

'No, please. Don't get me wrong. I know it is someone else. I just want to be sure it's this guy. The police seem happy to point the finger at anyone at the moment, including me.'

She looks at me, talking calmly, 'Look, I wasn't aware of this until just now, but forensics have put him at the scene, actually in the cottage, in the bedroom even, and, because of his past criminal record, his DNA was already on the police database.'

'So, they've had this information for what, over twenty-four hours, but decided not to inform me? Left me dangling as a suspect with a charge over my head? The bastards!'

'No. Don't look at it like that; try to remain calm; this is good news, and you should embrace it. You couldn't recall what happened, which didn't help your case. They have a new prime suspect now; this could be the man who killed Tanya and Craig. Confronted with the forensic evidence placing him there, he admitted to being at the scene. He has prior convictions for violent behaviour; he is known to the police and has connections to serious organised crime groups.'

This is excellent news, but I'm not feeling it, not yet. 'I know I should embrace it, but they thought it was me and dragged me over the coals over the last few days, formally arresting me and charging me.' Then it dawns on me what she just said. 'What do you mean he *could be the man*? He is, isn't he?' She doesn't answer immediately, and I can see there is something else. 'What is it? What are you not telling me?'

She places her right hand behind her neck, rotating her neck from front to back, then side to side, until I hear a slight click, all the while never removing her eyes from me. 'He admits to being there, in the room even, but he denies killing them.'

'What?'

'He is saying they were already dead when he entered the room.'

'What the...? I can't believe what I'm hearing. He must have done it, surely?'

'Well, the police are confident he did it and that he is just trying to evade the double murder charge. He knows the police can put him at the scene, which he's already admitted to, but it looks like he wants the police to *prove* that he killed them.'

'What can he possibly gain from this? A reduced sentence on mental capacity? What?'

'Well, the crimes he'll be charged with will depend on what the detectives can demonstrate and what the Crown Prosecution Service decide upon; it could be difficult to prove he killed them beyond a reasonable doubt.'

'Can you find out who this man is? I might know him; there may be something that I can add to help the police prove why he did this. If I or Melissa know him, we can help.'

'We can ask when DI Robbins comes in; I know the police have charged him, so we will get to know his name shortly, and then, I will get them to drop the charges against you.'

This is good news. But why would he murder them? And why leave us alone upstairs? My first thought is that we are lucky he crashed his car and survived so that we can get some answers and understand the motive behind this, but my thoughts soon turn to I wish he had died in the crash; it would probably save us all from a lot of aggravation and further pain that is to come. But they have him, and he's been charged; that's a relief.

The door opens, and DI Robbins walks in, all smiles. 'Good morning, Martin and Kaja. We have some good news.'

'So, I have just been hearing,' I reply without the courtesy of a return good morning and to the annoyance of both Robbins and Kaja, from their respective looks.

'Ah, OK. Well, yes, we have arrested and charged a man with the murder of Craig Tyler and your wife, Tanya.'

'When? When did you charge him?'

'Last evening. He is currently in hospital recovering from a car crash after fleeing the scene.'

'And you are only just telling me this now? A phone call last night would have been welcome. I came here this morning in the belief I am still your prime suspect and still under a charge of murder that I didn't do. As you can imagine, I didn't sleep well last night.'

My solicitor touches my forearm and looks at DI Robbins, 'Apologies, Detective. I am sure you can appreciate the pressure my client has been under and the concerns he has. Can you disclose the man's identity to us?'

Robbins coughs mildly and nods slightly, then looks at me. 'I apologise, Martin. You are quite right. I could have informed you last night, and I should have done. I am sorry.'

I feel awkward suddenly. They have the man who killed them, meaning I'm no longer a suspect, and I'm sitting here giving him a hard time. 'No, I'm sorry, it's me that should apologise for my behaviour and tone; I recognise you have a difficult job to do, and I'm not helping, and that is what I want to do, to help you.'

'OK, we're good; shall we start again?'

'Yes, let's. Good morning, Detective.'

'Good morning. The man we have charged is called Dimitri Hatzis. We have strong evidence that puts him at the cottage and in the bedroom where the deceased couple were found. We believe we have a motive for his actions, and we are investigating further to identify the person or persons who gave him his instructions.'

'His instructions? Do you mean they were murdered because someone else wanted them dead? What, like an assassination?'

'Yes, a contract kill or an organised crime gang hit. We'll know more after further interviews and investigation work, but we believe that your wife, Tanya, was probably in the wrong place at the wrong time; Hatzis possibly thought Tanya was Craig's wife, although, on that, we are speculating at the moment.'

'Jeez, oh my. Wrong place, wrong time. Tanya.'

We are all quiet for a few seconds until my solicitor breaks the silence.

'Detective, I presume you will then drop all charges against my client, and he is free to leave.'

'Yes, of course, all charges have been dropped.' Looking at me, he continues, 'Martin, we will be in touch as things progress, and my officers will keep you appraised of developments. Once again, I apologise for not contacting you at the earliest opportunity.'

DI Robbins is standing and holding out his right hand, wanting me to shake hands with him. I look at Kaja; she is already packing away her notepad and readying to leave. I stand up, and as I grasp his hand, a thought comes to mind. I ask him, whilst gripping his hand, 'So what about the attempted murder charge of Melissa, I mean? I was charged with that also. Has that been dropped?'

'Yes, all charges against you have been dropped.' He shakes my hand and then Kaja's in turn. 'Have a good day,' he says, leaving the interview room.

22

Martin - Tanya's Funeral

Wednesday, 16th August

It's been two months since they died, and Tanya's funeral was harder than I thought it would be. Tanya's family held it together exceptionally well under the circumstances, supporting each other, especially her mother; outwardly, she appeared strong, mainly collected, and organised, but I could tell, beneath it all, she was clearly struggling. There were times I saw her cry, joined by Tanya's father, which is only natural and to be expected; plenty did. Tanya's brother was exceptionally strong, providing a life and times eulogy for his little sister. I have always found it difficult to watch a man cry, tears clearly from emotional pain for a lost loved one, and when he cried, I could feel his grief deeply.

It was Tanya's previously discussed wish with her brother that she was to be buried and that it should be in the cemetery that wrapped itself around the small village church. This cemetery is the final resting place of several of Tanya's former relatives and ancestors, the family living in and around this village for over five generations.

Tanya's mother, my mother-in-law, invited Melissa to the funeral, but she declined. Given the nature of Tanya's death and the relationship Tanya had with her husband, I can appreciate why she would want to stay away. I had the same dilemma over Craig's funeral, and similarly, I didn't attend his.

Over the last hour or so, the mood and atmosphere at the family home have become much lighter. Children run around between parents and grandparents, sipping tea and eating triangular sandwiches and snacks. The patio doors are open, and family and friends have spilled out into the garden and sunshine.

I look at Tanya's parents; they are good people, kind, caring, and strong together. They've had to endure just as much as any of us through these last couple of months, and they have done so together, a couple supportive of and reliant on each other in equal measure.

Wandering through the living room and then the dining room, I familiarise myself with the family photos of Tanya and her brother growing up, posing with relatives, or photographs taken candidly when playing or writing, natural unposed shots, capturing the essence of them. There is so much love in this house, and even though it has been severely dented, I believe it will prevail.

Tanya's father approaches me with a glass in each hand of what I presume to be whisky. 'Martin, it's good to see you; you are more than welcome here any time.' He lifts one glass and offers it to me.

Taking it, I look at it as I swirl the contents. 'Thank you. That was a beautiful service. And I'm sorry I've been distant recently, since, you know… I've had some stuff to work through and come to terms with.'

'No apologies required, Martin. I can't really imagine what you've been going through. I know I would be lost without Tanya's mum, and for Tanya to be taken from us so young, well, it's just…' He sniffs and raises his glass, 'To our darling daughter and your beautiful wife.'

I raise my glass with him, and we each knock back the contents in one swallow. The whisky catches my throat slightly, and I cough. Looking at me, he smiles, putting his left arm around my shoulder, 'Come on, son, let's go outside.'

Standing at the lower end of the garden under a cherry tree in full fruit, he broaches the subject of the upcoming trial, 'Well, are you as confident as the police are that they have got their man?'

'Yes, I am,' I reply, 'as confident as anyone can be when the one accused will not confess. It's going to be all about the evidence, I suppose.'

'And, how good the lawyers are,' he adds.

'Yes, I suppose so. Are you not confident it's him then?'

'I am, yes, but I just want him to admit it. I want him to be an honourable man, to own up to what he has done, and to let us all know, without doubt, we have the right person.' The children are running around in the trees at the back of the house, laughing and playing tag, and as he watches them, he adds, 'Oh, to be innocent again, carefree, and full of hope.'

I look at him with a solemn expression, 'I know, but we do have the right man. He is guilty. He won't own up to it because I think he was ordered to kill Craig; Tanya was merely collateral damage in his eyes. But if he admits it was a hit, an assassination, then the police would turn their focus on the person that gave him the order.' As I'm saying this, there is a tone of frustration in my voice and delivery.

He looks at me and asks, 'How are you, Martin? I am sorry, I have never really asked you.'

'Angry. Yeah, I'm angry. Two young lives lost, taken, and so brutally. I don't think I'll ever fully get over it.'

'No, I know we won't; we lost our only daughter. Mercifully, our son and daughter-in-law have blessed us with two beautiful grandchildren, and we focus on them,' his eyes following the kids again around the garden.

'I was upstairs, unconscious; there was nothing I could do. I was no more than thirty yards away; why didn't I hear them? I could have done something.'

He turns back to me, taking a firm grip of the top of my right arm. 'Now don't do that, Martin. You can't blame yourself for what happened. It is not your fault.'

It's difficult to talk with him, as a slice of that inner anger relates to Tanya and Craig having an affair. He must know that, but still, I can't say that to him; he is such a decent, honest man, and what is done is done. There is no turning the clock back, so why add to the anguish we all feel.

'I know, but it's difficult not to feel guilty.'

23

Melissa – Crown Court, Lancaster

Friday Afternoon, 15th March

It's taken nine months from his arrest for his case to appear in court; the police wanted to run down different lines of inquiry, it seemed to exhaustion. Martin thought the police were hoping Hatzis would turn on his gang, but in the end, the CPS pushed ahead; everyone needed closure. Attending the court proceedings to hear the case against Hatzis is harrowing. Of course, I know Tanya and Craig were murdered, but I didn't fully appreciate the scene of their death. Martin and I initially attended court together, but after a couple of days of evidence, Martin thought it best that we didn't arrive, leave, or sit together during the trial. The reporters were having a field day outside the Court building, and he didn't want our friendship to become the subject of scandalous reporting. I struggled with his decision; I would have welcomed his support, but my father is wonderful, taking time away from work to be with me through this ordeal.

Over the last six months or so, since Tanya's funeral, Martin and I haven't spoken much, and probably on balance, we have communicated more using polite text messages and emails. I was hoping we could spend a bit of time together over Christmas, but he didn't want to. I was starting to get concerned for him as I thought he was slipping back into the illness he managed to overcome, but after speaking with him briefly just before New Year, he seemed fine, just wanting some space to get his life back on track, deciding what he wanted to do after this was all over.

At times, I glance a look across the public gallery to Martin and see him sitting with Tanya's parents, Tanya's mother almost always on the brink of tears. When photos of the crime scene were shown this morning during examination in chief, she looked away, averting her eyes in case she caught sight of them, burying her head into Martin's embrace. Martin is strong; he told me before the case started that he would face up to Tanya's killer, and he would not cower away. To be honest, I think if Martin could get some time alone with Hatzis, he would kill him… slowly, and I believe I would join him; anything to help assuage the silent guilt I carry.

The CPS and police are confident the jury will find him guilty, the sentence being a whole life tariff with a minimum of thirty years. We need to see justice done.

The judge adjourns the court for the day and the weekend, to restart on Monday morning. Hatzis is taken back down and, I presume, back to prison for the weekend. We file out of the court and head outside into bright sunshine, walking beneath trees around the Castle about to bud new growth, a setting of peace and tranquillity that belies the history of this place. Lancaster Castle, formerly a prison built around a Norman Keep, is now a museum and tourist attraction, but the Crown Court remains operational, it being the second oldest continuously functioning court in the country.

I see Martin with Tanya's parents heading towards the train station, in the opposite direction to where I'm heading. I've decided to stay the weekend in Lancaster, not for any real reason other than I didn't fancy the journey to and from Lancaster at the beginning and end of the week; the road traffic and the trains are unpredictable at best. I walk back to the Saracen's Head Inn in the city centre, where I have been staying all week during the trial. It's a quaint old English Inn with plenty of history and tales to tell; I can manage the low beams and sloping timber floors, but anyone over five feet ten inches tall would risk banging their head every few steps taken.

In my room, I drop onto the bed and close my eyes, thinking about nothing really, just wanting to drift away for a few moments. I can hear muffled sounds from the street below and voices along the corridor, comforting background noise to help me drift off to sleep.

My mobile phone rings on the bedside table, and I jump from the deeper sleep I'd fallen into. Looking at my watch, I've been asleep for nearly an hour. Picking up the phone and turning the screen towards me, I see its Martin. Do I answer it?

Of course, 'Hi Martin, you must be nearly home by now. Is everything OK?'

'Yes, fine, although I didn't go home, I accompanied Tanya's parents to the train station and saw them off. No, I'm staying in Lancaster this weekend. Are you back home now?'

'Hah, no, I'm staying in Lancaster too. I've never been here before and just thought, rather than travel, I'd just chill here for the weekend.'

'Oh, well, then, we're both at loose ends in the city; do you fancy dinner tonight, or maybe just a few drinks?'

I wasn't expecting this, 'Will it be OK? I mean, with the Press and everything, you were worried they'd make something of the two of us being together at the trial.'

'I know a couple of quiet places just on the edge of the city centre, down by the river; we'll be fine down there; I wouldn't expect there to be anyone down there showing us any interest.'

'Well then, yes, that will be nice. I've not eaten yet, so something to eat would be good.'

'Right then, I know just the place. Where are you staying? I will come over, and we can walk down together.'

'I'm in the Saracen's Head, on Market Street. Shall we say seven thirty in the bar?'

'That sounds good, OK, seven thirty it is then. See you shortly.'

'Bye, Martin,' and the call finishes. I stare at the phone in my hand and wonder if I'm doing the right thing. We're in the middle of the trial, in the city where it's being held, with our former spouses being at the centre of that trial. I know this isn't London or Manchester, and it's relatively small and quiet for a city, but still, should we? I swing my legs off the bed, my answer made, and head for the bathroom. It'll be good to be with Martin again, just the two of us.

Just before seven thirty, I'm in the bar with two drinks, sitting in a small corner booth. Martin walks in through the front door, bending at the knees slightly and lowering his head to miss the top of the door frame. I watch him trying to stand upright, but the lower oak beams make it difficult for him. Looking around, he spots me smiling at him, and he walks with a lowered head and cowered shoulders, slipping into the wooden bench seat opposite me, saying as he sits, 'Well, this is snug,' smiling back at me.

'It is, I like it. I got you a G&T to start with. Is that OK?'

'Yes, yes, that's fine, thank you. It is good to see you, Melissa.' Looking directly into my eyes, he raises his glass, and we clink with a cheers, although as soon as we say it, it's clear we both feel uncomfortable about it on such a day.

As I place my glass back on the table, he continues, 'Now, let's make a pact. There will be no talk of the trial this evening. We're just two friends catching up. Deal?'

'Yes, deal. I wish I could put it all behind me as though it never happened.'

'Well, it'll soon be done, and we can try to get on with life. That's it, for now, no more trial talk.'

He's smiling at me, his blue eyes bright and kind but surrounded by a tired and worn complexion. I reach for his hand, placing mine on top of his, and we look at each other, old friends who have each lost something precious in a most grotesque way. I tap the back of his hand and pull mine away, 'Now then, what is this little restaurant you know of, and how did you come across it?'

24

Dimitri – HMP Witchull

Early Friday Evening, 15th March

This is all going too far now. I must stop this somehow. The trouble is, the only way I can think of involves grassing on Nico Costas to save my own skin, and that'll make me a dead man walking for sure.

There's no way I can spend the rest of my life in a place like this; that last four-year stretch was enough for me. A grass, though, me? But what have they done to help me out of this mess? Nothing other than pay for my solicitor and barrister, and I know I should be grateful, but this is easily a minimum thirty-year stretch, and the evidence against me will get me there. Paying for my legal team is one thing, but why should that buy my silence, especially if I'm going to get life? What good is it going to do me?

The prison van pulls up outside Witchull in the dark, and I can hear the gates opening. I won't be hearing them open for much longer, well, not from outside of the walls, that is. Rubbing my head against the cold steel panel, I'm struggling with this. If I try to do a deal now, would the judge take it into account? Could I get out under a witness protection scheme? The amount of stuff I know about Nico Costas has got to be worth something, something I can barter with, but it's worth nothing if I'm still inside; they can easily get to me in here.

Inside the inner gates, the van stops, and the doors are unlocked; only three passengers travelling in the play bus today. Stepping down, I look to the prison officer with the clipboard and ask, 'Here, Boss, any chance before I go back to my cell, I can make a call to my solicitor, please? It is quite urgent; it's about the trial. There is something I want to ask him which might be of interest to the judge.'

'Do I look like your social secretary, Hatzis?'

'No. Sorry, it is urgent, though.' He tuts and writes something on his clipboard.

'OK, I'll ask. But if you're screwing me around, you'll spend the weekend in solitary. Got it?'

'Sure, but I'm not screwing around; I think the judge will be interested in this.' The prisoner in front of me turns his head and eyeballs me, spitting on the floor, and I stare him down.

The prison officer goes straight for the prisoner, 'Hey, you scruffy bastard, no more of that, or you'll be solitary next door to him. You understand? I said, do you understand?'

'Yeh.' He sniffs hard, turning his head back, and continues shuffling in through the narrow stone doorway.

On the inside, we walk through the Reception Area and into the side room to be searched, the usual joy. When I reappear, one of the prison officers informs me I can make a call to my solicitor, and he takes me to another room with a wall phone below a high window. 'Make it quick, Hatzis; I want to get home to my missus, my beer, my dinner and my T.V.'

'Sure, Boss, as quick as I can,' I say politely, all the time thinking I would love to put my right foot in contact with his face. Punching in my call PIN number, I dial my solicitor's mobile number; it's not the cheapest call I'll make, but it's probably the only one he'll answer at this time of day. It connects.

'Yeh, Mr Waiting, it's Dimitri Hatzis. I'm back at Witchull. I need to talk with you about an urgent matter.'

'Oh, yes, what is it?'

I move in close to the wall and talk quietly; I don't want to be overheard. 'I want to do a deal. I know stuff which will get me out of here, you know, witness protection level stuff.'

'Not on the phone, Dimitri. I'll make arrangements to come over to see you. Don't say anything to anyone until we sort out the deal. You got it?'

'Yeh, I got it. Cheers.'

25

Martin – The Spice Merchant, Lancaster

Friday Night, 15th March

I don't think I've enjoyed an evening as much in a long time, for obvious reasons. Melissa is charming and witty, and if I didn't know any better, it's as though she has not lived through the same trauma as me. I know this is brief escapism, and reality will hit us soon enough, but we are enjoying ourselves in each other's company in the moment. She talks of things with a passion, and I'd say she is looking forward rather than backward, thinking of a future after the trial.

Dinner was great; I love this little restaurant overlooking the River Lune. I managed to reserve one of the secluded alcove tables at the rear of the restaurant, giving us the privacy we wanted but with the ability to still feel the atmosphere of the place. I settle the bill, with Melissa being adamant we should half it but, as this was my idea, I pay.

Stepping outside onto the quayside, Melissa links my arm, and we walk quietly along the waterfront. The sun has settled behind us, and what little warmth of the day there was, has ebbed in unison with the tide in the Lune. We are not talking, just enjoying each other's company; no hassle, no pressures, no worries, nothing to dictate what we have to do this evening or this weekend.

We follow the Lune for about half a mile, then turn in towards the city centre. Even though I am enjoying Melissa's company and this evening so much, I cannot, and will not, take advantage of the situation. At the end of Market Street, I stop and look at Melissa. 'I really enjoyed this evening; I'm so glad we both stayed up here in Lancaster this weekend.'

'Me too,' she replies, and without hesitation, she rises on tiptoe and kisses me on the lips. In that brief second, an electricity, a passion runs through me that I've not felt for a very long time. I want more, but as I go to put my hands to her face, Melissa pulls away abruptly, displaying shock on her face. 'I'm so sorry, I shouldn't have done that.' She looks down to one side, breaking her look at me.

I put my hands to her shoulders and then to her head, raising her chin to look at me, 'There is nothing to be sorry for.'

'No, I just shouldn't have. Sorry.' She turns and walks away briskly, heading towards the Inn where she is staying.

'Melissa,' I call out, but she carries on and disappears through the low door to the Inn.

Standing there looking down the street, I must look like I'm lost to anyone passing by, and I suppose, inside, I am. Could something good come out of the awful events that have happened, the two of us finding each other? Are we meant to be together, or is it just that we know each other as old friends, and our normal reserve has relaxed because we each seek companionship?

After a minute or so, I set off walking towards my hotel. The two of us being together feels good to me, although if we did get together in that way, we'd only be reminded of our past and their murders every day we look at each other. There is a tug of war in my head, balancing reason with desire, and reason wins out. No, it won't work, don't be silly, you fool, it'll be too complicated. But this is awkward now; we'll need to clear the air between us and remain friends as always intended. Deciding to let her sleep tonight, I will call her tomorrow to put things back as they were, or will the desire side pull at me, hoping she will want more? Will she want more of me after she's slept on it?

I need a drink.

26

Melissa – Lancaster

Saturday Morning, 16th March

What was I thinking of last night? I shouldn't have done that. Martin has lost his wife in the most grotesque way, and all I can think about is me. For god's sake, I lost my husband as well; was it the wine taking over last night, or do I want more from Martin?

As I'm finishing breakfast in the small dining room at the rear of the Inn, I decide I need to speak with Martin as we can't leave it like we did last night. We are friends, no more than that.

'Would you like anything else?' asks the server.

'Err, no, thank you; that was very nice; I really enjoyed it. Oh well, maybe another pot of tea, if I could, please?'

'Yes, of course, I'll bring it right over.'

He turns, heading back to the kitchen, when my mobile phone rings. Fishing my handset out of my bag, the screen shows it's Martin calling. Ah, I should answer this, but I'm not sure what to say. Do I answer it or not? Then it stops ringing on the fourth ring; the decision is made for me. Maybe he's not sure what to do, what to say, he doesn't want to push things, I don't know. What I do know, however, is that we should stay good friends, but even as I'm thinking this, I'm torn; I thought I knew what I wanted until he phoned me.

The server reappears with the fresh pot of tea and places it on the table.

'Thank you.'

Looking back down at my phone, I need to decide what to do. We do need to talk, to talk this through and clear up any confusion I created last night with that kiss. I'll text him a message to meet this afternoon, and we can sort this out, as I do want Martin in my life. I've always liked him and enjoyed his company, and I don't want to lose him too; I struggle at times to understand or appreciate why Tanya had an affair behind his back. I know Craig was always a bit of a player, and after years of denial, I have come to acknowledge it and admit it to myself, but Tanya and Martin were always strong together. How the hell could I have let this happen? This went further than it should have. The wave of guilt starts to roll over me again, and as I go to pick up the teapot, my shaking hand makes the pot lid rattle gently. Come on, girl, calm yourself.

Placing the teapot down, I pick up the phone and start typing a text message: "*Hi Martin, we should meet up and talk through what happened last night*" and press send.

I pour that cup of tea, and when adding milk, my phone pings; it's Martin replying; that was quick.

"*Yes. Let's meet at the Ashton Memorial today, say 1pm?*"

I text back a short and simple "*Yes.*" I have no idea where the Memorial is, but it sounds like it won't be hard to find.

What would Tanya's parents and family think if Martin and I were to get together? Then, questioning myself, why is that my problem? I shouldn't be thinking of how they might feel when it's my life I should be thinking of. My mind is spiralling now, twisting a downward dive and then looping back up again. Why am I thinking about how Tanya's family would feel? After all, it was their daughter who cheated on Martin and had an affair with my husband. If Martin and I remain friends, it won't be a problem; it's only a problem if we become more than good friends and I've decided we shouldn't go there.

I finish my tea, leave the table, exit the Inn, and start to walk the streets of this small city centre. I need something else to occupy my mind, and all I can think to do right now is wander through the shops and try some retail therapy, while keeping an eye open for any Ashton Memorial signs.

27

Martin – The Ashton Memorial, Lancaster

Saturday Afternoon, 16th March

Walking across the city centre and up through Williamson Park has helped me work through what I want to say to Melissa. We should remain friends; that is clear to me. No complications or accusations of abandoning the memories and relationships we had with our respective spouses recently departed. The thought went through my mind this morning that someone could even think we had something to do with Tanya and Craig's deaths, having a hand in the proceedings so that we could then be together. Even if friends and family don't consider it, I'm sure some cynical police officer or venomous reporter will, and then this whole thing could be raked up again.

Friends, just good friends.

Sitting on the top step of the granite stairs rising to the Memorial, I look out across the park below. The good weather has brought out families and individuals, joggers and dog walkers, all having a good time enjoying this unusual warm spell so early in spring. I spot Melissa in the park, walking up to meet me, and I stand and raise my right arm, a simple wave, trying to catch her attention; she sees me and acknowledges with a small wave in return and enters the left-hand set of granite steps climbing to meet me.

When she reaches me, she is a little out of breath and turns to admire the vista in front of us. 'Wow, I didn't think we would have a view like this. Is that the sea?'

'Yes, and to your right, the southern hills of the Lake District.' There is definitely an air of nervousness between the two of us; I sound like a tour guide, and Melissa, a keen tourist, both being polite and not sure how to broach what happened. I start, 'About last night,' just as Melissa speaks.

'I'm sorry about…'

The ice is broken. We both show relief and laugh. 'Friends?' I suggest, smiling.

'Yes, friends,' and we hug.

'Come on, let's walk and talk, shall we?'

For the next couple of hours or so, we talk about last night, how we each felt, and the emotions being stirred up. What becomes clear to me is that we do have more in common than we first thought, not just the earlier friendship and the untimely deaths of our two partners but also the general likes and dislikes of music, films, books, food, and holiday destinations; rekindling our discussions of maybe visiting New York.

I buy a couple of ice creams for us, and we slowly head downhill again towards the city centre. Inevitably, we start to talk about Hatzis and the trial.

'He will be found guilty, won't he?' Melissa asks.

'Yes, I believe so. After this first week, everyone is convinced; listening to the evidence against him is compelling.'

'Do you think it was a hit by this organised crime family?'

'I'm not sure, but it's looking like that, although without a confession from Hatzis, the police are unable to prove it. Hatzis is the key to all this. It's clear he did it, but the reason why if it's not related to the family isn't so clear.'

'The police suggested to me once that there may have been something between Tanya and Hatzis, but I can't see it myself, can you?'

'No. The charge of murder will stick; whether or not he'll tell us why he did it, only time will tell.'

'To kill them like that, though; whatever possessed him?'

The crime scene images flash across my mind again, and suddenly, I've lost my interest in the ice cream. 'I don't know, and we'll probably never know.' I want to change the subject now. 'Shall we dare have dinner again tonight?'

She coughs a little into her ice cream and turns to look at me. 'You want to risk it? You do know I struggle to keep my hands off you, you know that, don't you?' and laughs.

'Well, I'll risk it, if you will.'

'OK, let's do it, only tonight is my treat; I'm paying.'

'Well, how can a man refuse an invitation like that?'

28

Dimitri – HMP Witchull

Saturday Evening, 16th March

Lying on my bunk, with the door open, the noise of the prison echoing outside, I read the book I picked from the prison library, The Count of Monte Cristo. I'm not really getting into it; the film will probably be better. My cell door swings open slowly, and I look up to see three real heavies enter, the last one closing the door almost shut behind him.

I swing my legs out from the bunk, intending to stand up. 'Alright, guys, what's occurring?'

'We have a message from Mr Costas.' This stops me.

'What do you mean?' Why does it take three of you to deliver a message?' And I know the instant I say it, I'm in trouble here, someone has told him. 'I'm good, honest, I won't say anything, I'm loyal.'

The two in the middle of my cell reach down and grab me by my arms, pulling me out of the bunk and standing me up to face the guy with his back to the door. 'What's… what's the message?' I ask, trying not to show I'm terrified.

'Mr Costas thought you were a good soldier; he didn't believe you would turn on him.'

'I've not. I am a good soldier.'

'Who the fuck do you think is paying for your solicitor? Did you not think there was a reason Mr Costas would pay his fees? Mr Costas has decided you're a liability now, and he doesn't like taking risks he can't control. You deserve what's coming to you, grass.'

'What? I didn't…'

He walks quickly up to me whilst one of the guys puts his arm around my neck, locking it in a hold. Message Man forces my mouth open and pushes in a wet rag, shoving it hard, and I start to cough and gag. He turns to pick up my grey sweatpants off the table, throwing the seat of the pants over my head, around the back of my head and tying the legs in a crude knot over the wet rag in my mouth. As much as I try, I can't make a noise other than a low moan or grunt. They jostle me backwards to the bunk bed frame, and Messenger Man pulls a piece of steel wire from his pocket, lashes it to the bunk frame, and then ties it around my neck. Now I know what the message is.

'Mr Costas sends his regards and expects you to set a good example of what happens to a grass.'

He kicks me hard between my legs, and I crumple; the wire bites hard into my neck, cutting in, slowly garrotting me, and I try to stand up again. I get a full punch into my stomach, and I'm struggling to breathe. He grabs my head and looks into my eyes with burning evil.

'They'll all know you were a grass, and they'll see what happens to a grass in here.'

The other two each grab one of my ankles, and forcing my knees to bend, they raise my feet up behind me. The full weight of my body now rests on the thin wire wrapped around my neck, slowly cutting into my throat. I scratch with my fingers at the wire, now already burying itself into my flesh. Message Man stares into my wide-open eyes, smiling, enjoying this. The wire is cutting deeper, the pain is unbearable, I can't scream or call out, I can't breathe. They lift my ankles higher, and I feel warm blood running down onto my chest, and I start to black out. He is laughing only a few inches from my face as my vision gets narrower, going darker, and my arms drop limp.

29

Martin – The Royal Arms Hotel, Lancaster

Sunday Morning, 17th March

Lying in my double bed, listening to the peal of church bells ring out over the quiet streets, I mull over how enjoyable yesterday and last night were. To escape our real lives, even if just for this weekend, has been a wonderful release for me, and I think also for Melissa. We have another easy day planned with a nice Sunday roast together this afternoon, both of us avoiding the inevitable return to Crown Court tomorrow morning.

I've come to realise that being with Melissa has allowed me to set to one side what has happened, even though it impacted and affected us both equally. Well, maybe not quite equally; Melissa wasn't charged with double murder and attempted murder or had to endure the pressure of formal police interviews. Thinking back to that time, I still feel as though I have unsettled business with the police. I know violent crime has a higher statistical probability of involving a family member or a partner, but their trying to pin the murder charges on me was unacceptable. I know I have to stop thinking like this: that was then, and this is now; this is all going to be resolved in the next couple of weeks when the trial concludes, and then we can put it behind us.

I brought my running gear with me this weekend, thinking I would get some use out of it; all part of my trying to get back into trim again. I've just got to muster up the drive to get out of bed, put it on, and get out there. Yep, come on, Marty Boy, let's do it.

Getting out of bed, I place my feet on the woven rug and reach over for my kit bag from the chair. Unzipping the bag, I pull out my running shirt, and as I pull it over my head, my mobile rings. That'll be Melissa, and I eagerly pull the shirt down, reach for the phone, and hit open.

'Hi, good morning,' saying without checking the screen, an instant mistake when I hear his voice.

'Oh. Good morning, Martin. Detective Inspector Robbins here.'

'Ah, oh, sorry, Detective Inspector, I was expecting a different caller. Er, what can I do for you.'

'I have some news for you.'

'Oh, good news, I hope?'

'Yes, well, it depends on your point of view, I suppose.'

'This sounds a little ominous; what is it, Inspector?'

'It's relating to Dimitri Hatzis. He was found dead last night in his prison cell at HMP Witchull.'

'Dead?'

'Yes. The local police are investigating it, but they informed me this morning it was made to look like suicide, but they strongly suspect that he was killed, murdered.'

'Oh my god. So, what does that mean now? He'll still be found guilty, won't he?'

'No, I'm afraid not. The court case will stop, and his case, along with any prospect of a conviction, will be dismissed as moot.'

'What? No! He is guilty. We need a guilty verdict for closure, Inspector.'

'I'm afraid that won't be possible. We will attend court tomorrow morning, but I expect the Judge to dismiss the case. He's no longer alive, so there is no one to stand trial. I'm sorry.'

'Well, who killed him?'

'We don't know yet. But that will be investigated by the local police; it doesn't fall within my patch. Look, I wanted to let you know straight away. You have a right to know, and you won't need to travel back up to Lancaster tomorrow. It'll all just be formal procedure to dismiss the case.'

This news has floored me; I needed that guilty conviction. 'Does Melissa, er, Mrs Tyler know? Have you called her?'

'No, not yet. I tried her mobile number before calling you. She didn't answer. I've left a message for her to call me back.' He clearly hears my deep sigh. 'Look, Martin, I've probably said more than I should have. Please keep a lid on this if you can for the time being. I need to speak with Tanya's parents as well.'

'Do you want me to call them, tell them? We are close.'

'No, I'll inform them officially. But thank you, that is kind of you; tough news like this is never welcome.'

'Will we ever know why he killed them then?'

'No, probably not, but we maintain he was given an order from the Costas family, relating to the Insurance claim. That line of enquiry continues, but it'll be weaker now as the main corroborator is now dead.'

'Shit,' just slipped out of my mouth, 'Oh, I'm sorry.'

'No, no, you have no need to be sorry. That was my first reaction when I was informed early this morning.'

'I'll be in court in the morning. I stayed up here in Lancaster. Will you be there?'

'I'm not sure yet. From our perspective, this case is closed. The CPS will follow the Judge's instructions, and that'll be it. I'm sorry, Martin, that you and your families won't get to see him convicted.'

'Well, Detective, from my perspective, I suppose justice has been served, just not in a way we all expected.'

'Yes, well. If I do attend court in the morning, we'll have a chat afterwards. If not, I'll call you to let you know what we intend to do. But I think it's safe to say, with budget and manpower constraints, we'll be closing this down quickly after tomorrow, assuming the Judge dismisses the case.'

'OK. Wow, I'm not sure what to think.' I pause slightly, thinking of Melissa rather than Robbins. 'Thank you for letting me know, Inspector.'

'Not a problem. I'm sorry for disturbing you on a Sunday with such news.'

'Not at all. Thank you, Inspector.'

The call ends, and I look at the screen before throwing my phone down onto the bed and following it, falling backwards with my hands to my face, covering my eyes. 'What the…' I say to myself.

Melissa.

Should I call her? Go to her? I'd best let Robbins inform her first. Getting dressed and heading over to the Saracen's Head is probably the best I can do for now; at least I'll be there not long after she finds out.

30

Melissa – Crown Court, Lancaster

Monday morning, 18th March

Considering that very few needed to be here today, we are all back in Crown Court this morning. We all planned to be here, and we all said we would see it through to the end. When I called DI Robbins back yesterday, he informed me of what had happened to Hatzis, but I didn't know what to think. My first reaction was to call Martin, and he was in my room within minutes of my call; we just hugged. He knew I would need support, and he was there, waiting for me to call him.

It's done now, I suppose. The courtroom is buzzing with chatter, awaiting the Judge to appear. The public gallery is full; I suppose this is an unusual occurrence, especially for such a high-profile double murder case.

Dad came up on the early train, and we had breakfast together. He's happy that Hatzis is dead, and the trial will end today, with no need for further testimony, examination, or disturbing photographs. Dad was never a big fan of Craig, but he put up with him because he was my husband, my choice of the man I wanted to be with. I don't think Dad was surprised by Craig having extramarital affairs though, just surprised he had the audacity to have one with Tanya, my friend.

I can see Tanya's parents also travelled up, and Martin is sitting with them. Tanya's mother looks more relaxed than she was last week; again, she is probably relieved it will all be over with shortly.

'All rise,' calls out the bailiff.

The Judge enters and takes his place.

Within a few minutes, the formalities are over. As there is no co-defendant, no one else on trial, and the only defendant has since died, the Judge dismisses the case and discharges the jury.

Walking out of the courtroom's public gallery, Martin catches me looking at him and gently nods while guiding his former mother-in-law to the exit. It seems like he is satisfied with the outcome, well, as satisfied as anyone could be in such circumstances. My father and I follow Martin and his in-laws down the stone steps to the front foyer, out into the bright sunshine and the waiting media. After some cajoling from the media pack, Martin agrees to speak to the cameras. He stands stoically, extracting a folded piece of paper from his inside pocket.

'Tanya was my beautiful wife of four years. Craig was the best friend a man could have. They were murdered by Dimitri Hatzis, and although we have been denied a guilty verdict, whichever way I look at this, I believe justice has been done. On behalf of the families and friends of Tanya and Craig, I thank you for your support during these difficult months and now ask you to kindly respect our privacy and provide us some quiet time to reflect and consider these events. We thank the police for their diligent investigation work and the Crown Prosecution Service for bringing this case to court. For us, Tanya and Craig's family and friends, Hatzis is guilty of double murder as charged; we don't need a jury to decide that. Thank you.'

Martin folds the paper, tucking it back inside his jacket, and takes a couple of steps backwards. There is a question called out from a reporter, 'Martin, Martin. Did you know about Tanya and Craig's affair?'

I can't quite believe a question like that would be asked on a day like this, but I suppose that's the media for you. I look at Martin, and I can see his annoyance by the slight grimace on his face, but he doesn't outwardly react or respond.

The reporter calls out again, although this time directed to me, 'Melissa. Did you know about the affair?'

My father pulls me into his side, lowering his head slightly, 'Come on, love, let's get away from here.' I nod quickly, and we turn, heading away from the crowd and cameras.

Another reporter pops out in front of us, 'Are you satisfied with the outcome, Melissa?' and it's my father who replies.

'Yes, we are. Thank you. Now, please step aside.'

'It must have been awful to find out they were downstairs having sex while you were upstairs, unconscious after being drugged by them. Any comment?'

Without breaking his stride, Dad knocks the recording device out of the reporter's hand, watching it hit the paved floor and accidentally kicking it under the feet of others in the mass. 'Oops,' he says, whilst looking directly at the reporter, 'Sorry about that, all this jostling, these crowds, you know how it is.'

The reporter bends down to search for his recorder, and we walk away at pace, down Castle Park and Castle Hill, towards the city centre, blending in with office types and shoppers going about their business.

31

Melissa – The Church of St Edward the Confessor

Friday, 12th April

Standing outside the small village church, watching people slowly enter, with my right hand resting on the top bar of the small timber gate, I'm really struggling with the thought of attending this memorial service. With the Court case now abandoned and behind us, Tanya's parents thought this service appropriate as a celebration of Tanya's life, hoping that the brutality of the events over the last ten months could be eased by bringing family and friends closer together once again. But Tanya and my husband, Craig, were having an affair; we all know this now. There is no escaping the fact that Craig and Tanya died in each other's arms in the act of lovemaking whilst Martin and I were asleep upstairs, unaware of what was happening downstairs. It seems that Tanya's parents are happy to whitewash over that little fact, but the reality is that if they weren't having an affair, Tanya would more than likely be alive today. It dawned on me some weeks ago that Hatzis was happy to kill two people in the way he did, but if Craig had been faithful to me, then it could easily have been me who was murdered with him that night or any other night.

But it's not the affair that is preventing me from opening the gate; it's the guilt, gnawing away at me inside still, a guilt I can never own up to, never discuss with anyone, something that will accompany me to my distant grave, unless it gets me there sooner. I shouldn't have done it.

'Are you as uneasy about this as I am?' the voice quietly whispers from behind me, startling me to a jolt. 'Sorry, I didn't mean to surprise you.'

As I turn, I look up and into Martin's eyes; he is calm, with a soft, apologetic smile, reaching out to touch my left arm.

'Oh, er, no.'

'No, that you are not uneasy about this, or no, that I didn't surprise you?'

'Then I should say yes to both. I'm sorry, I know it's awful to say this, but I'm not sure I want to celebrate the life of a woman who I thought of as a dear friend but who in reality was having an illicit affair with my husband.'

'But you came anyway?'

'Yes. I think I'm here to exorcise this guilt I'm carrying.' Oh my god, why did I just say that, and to Martin of all people?

'Guilt. Umm,' he shrugs, 'I know, survivor's guilt, my doctor calls it.'

Grasping at this, 'Oh, you too? That's a relief.' He moves closes to me, putting his arms around me, allowing me to turn and place my head on his chest. His embrace is comforting. I love Martin as a dear friend, and I have missed our conversations and time together. He is a gentle man, a strong man with a deeply caring side. I feel his chest rise, taking in air and then slowly releasing it through a deep, slow exhale.

'Well then, shall we go in, or shall we leave?' He slowly relaxes his arms, but I don't want to let go of his embrace. It's the first time I have felt genuine affection since that weekend with someone who can fully appreciate my pain and the guilt I feel.

I ponder the question for a moment, tugging at my emotions, then decide, 'Yes, I think we should go in. Somebody will have seen us, and it would look odd now if we didn't go in.'

'Yes, perhaps you're right.' I feel him lower his right arm behind me, swinging the gate open. 'Shall we? After you.'

We walk through the gate, and without thinking, we link arms as we slowly walk the uneven flagstone path to the open studded oak door of the small mediaeval church. As we reach the door, he whispers, 'We can do this, we're strong, we are survivors, we're together.'

On entering, the church seems full of people, a large turnout, but then again, it is a tiny church. Looking around for a place to sit, Martin insists I join him and Tanya's close family at the front. Everyone is kind and inviting, moving along the pew, making some space for me. The service is poignant yet witty at times, with family members and friends speaking of Tanya, remembering her as a child, through her teenage years, and into womanhood. I laugh, and I cry, and by the end of the service, I feel a relief, a lightening of an invisible load; it was as if we all used the opportunity collectively to remember and say goodbye to Tanya, and I am swept along with it. As the vicar passes through the congregation, Martin is thanking people, and I fall in with him, shaking hands and hugging people, some of whom I have never met before; this is what group therapy must be like is going through my mind, and it's working.

'We are going back to Tanya's parents' house, close family and friends. Would you like to join us?' Martin asks in a hushed voice.

'Err...' I wasn't expecting this; he's caught me off guard. 'No, thanks, I think it's best I don't.'

'I'll be there; we can talk.'

'No thanks, it'll be… awkward.'

'Why awkward?'

This is the reason why I thought I shouldn't be here today. 'Because it was my husband she was killed with.'

'Well, that's not your fault, is it?'

'No, but if they weren't having an affair, I'd be the one dead now; someone will say it; if not, they'll be thinking it. They lost their beautiful daughter, niece, and auntie because I wasn't the one in that bed with Craig when Hatzis entered.'

He looks at me and slightly tilts his head, 'Now, come on, you can't be thinking like that.'

'But I do. I feel guilty,' and as I say it, only I know there is more to my guilt. The good work done over the last hour has just left by the open oak door with the rest of the congregation, and I'm left with the heavy guilt feeling again.

'Don't be silly,' Martin says, trying to be kind, but it doesn't work with me; in fact, it has the opposite effect.

'No, I'm sorry. I'm leaving now,' turning and walking briskly down the aisle toward the font at the rear and the door to the left. Martin doesn't follow me, and I make my way between people milling around outside the church, through the gate, and cross the lane to my parked car. Once inside, I close the door and start to cry. Why did I come here today? I'll never be free of this.

32

Martin – Tanya's Memorial Service

What was all that about? I get that she is nervous, maybe concerned about what some may think of her being here today, but she was fine one second and then couldn't wait to get away from here as though the place was on fire. Or is it me? No, I don't see it. We were all very good friends, and I know there's been a tragedy, but two of us survived it, and we should be stronger together.

Tanya's brother approaches me and asks, 'Is everything alright, Martin? Melissa left in a hurry, then?'

'Yes, I think so. It's not a problem with the service or the people; it's… well, I think she is still having a tough time about it all. She lost her husband and a very dear friend, coupled with how they died and were found. I must admit, I still struggle processing it all at times.'

'It's only been, what, nearly ten months; come on, you need to give yourself a break. It could have been a lot worse. You were both lucky he didn't know you two were upstairs asleep.'

'I know, but…' I can feel the emptiness inside, and suddenly, tears well up in me.

He throws his arm around my shoulder and pulls me in tight, 'You're a good brother-in-law, Martin, and you always will be to me. What has happened has happened; there's no changing history, you know that. That bastard was locked up and would have been for the rest of his life if the trial had not stopped; I'm glad someone in there took a dislike to him and cut his time in prison short. Good riddance, it saved the taxpayers a lot of money, and we got closure.'

As he's saying this, I can feel the rage still in him, oozing out like a thousand shards. He also thinks Hatzis was murdered even though the official line is suicide; maybe someone in the police said something quietly to the family. We have all suffered from this and will continue to, and I turn and throw my arms around him, hugging him tight. I never really had a whole family to speak of, and I feel more like a part of Tanya's family than I ever could be with my own.

He pats me on my back a couple of times, and we move apart. 'Come on, back to the house. Mother Hen will be upset if you don't come back; she needs something to cluck over, and besides, I have a decent single malt for us to break open.'

He has me now, 'OK, I'll follow you over.' He nods, and I watch him leave the church, and for a few moments, I have the place to myself: it's so peaceful. Looking up at the stained-glass window that has been there for nearly three hundred years, the spring sunlight passing through emits coloured beams across the floor of the nave and the altar; it's been there a long time and will continue to be; a public symbol that the circle of life and death continues, regardless.

Can a place like this ease the guilt one carries?

33

Melissa - Martin's Bothy

Wednesday, 24th April

I'm not sure how he will react to me just turning up unannounced like this after nearly two weeks of avoiding his calls and messages; I'm hoping he can put my behaviour aside and be pleased to see me. Our last conversation was not the best, and I don't want to leave it like that, in fact, I now know I want more. We could be good for each other and good together. We've lived through the same trauma, experienced the accusations and intrusions into our personal lives and the comments of family members and friends, but what do they know, really? What can they possibly know not having gone through those experiences and had the same happen to them?

I'd forgotten how remote his Bothy is; the road up and around Kielder Water has hardly any vehicles on it, especially at this time of day when the sun is low, looking to fall behind pine forests and hills to the west. I cross the English-Scottish border, and instantly, I am surrounded by tall pine trees in a managed plantation. The road width drops to a single carriageway with vehicle passing places and, slowing, I recall that the turn-off is just a few hundred yards past the blue "Welcome to the Scottish Borders" sign. The turn-off to my right is onto a narrow stone track, and I crawl along, keeping my tyres aligned with the parallel gravel tracks. The twists and turns in the forest make this a truly remote place, and as I break through the far side of the woods, I see his Bothy in front, to the right of the track.

His Land Rover is parked at the side, beside the stone chimney breast, expelling a thin, wispy trail of smoke to the clear blue sky, slowly rising vertically. Turning to park my car alongside his, the front door of the old Bothy opens, and Martin is standing there with his arms folded, his body language indicating this is possibly not the good idea I thought it to be.

By the time I switch the engine off, Martin is standing by the driver's door, and he opens it.

'Hello, and what are you doing here? Have you lost your way?'

'Hi, well, yes, I was passing and thought I'd drop in,' showing a cheeky smile trying to disarm the situation.

'Oh, you often drive about thirty miles from a decent road, do you, up here in the Scottish Borders, a hundred and fifty miles from home. It's a good job I'm home then.' His smile is welcoming and a relief. I know I shouldn't have interrupted him in his work, but I had to see him without all the usual distractions. I step out of my car and stand upright in front of him, smiling. He throws his arms around me, and we hug tightly, each feeling the warmth of old friends reunited.

As we release, I look up into his face, 'I was a little worried I wouldn't be welcome,'

'Nonsense, you are always welcome,' and he kisses me on my cheek. 'And there's me thinking you didn't want to know me anymore. Have you got any bags with you, passerby?'

'Yes, I have, and some treats.'

'Ah, beware a woman bearing gifts.'

'No, nothing to hide, no agenda. I just wanted to spend some time with you to apologise and thought I'd surprise you,' I reply, watching the smile grow across his face.

'It is a nice surprise. Come on, let's get your things inside; it'll be dark soon.'

I lift the tailgate and reach in, pulling out my small suitcase and duffle bag. As I step back, he lifts the shopping bags, and we take them inside.

It's as I remember it, one large room comprising a living area and kitchen, a door opposite the fireplace to the one bedroom and another door to the small bathroom. That's it, simple and rustic. Martin places the shopping bags on the wooden table beside his laptop and notepads and starts to empty the contents, placing some foodstuffs in the fridge and others on the worktop beside the sink. He lifts out the bottle of single malt whisky and whistles softly, 'Umm, my favourite.' He turns to me, 'You remembered.'

'Yes, I thought I could use it to calm you down if I was in trouble for turning up on your doorstep.'

'Haha, you know me well. So, you did bring a gift with a hidden purpose?'

'I suppose I did,' smiling at him. 'Is it OK if I put my bags here,' indicating to the side of his well-worn, brown leather settee.

'Nonsense. You take the bedroom; the sheets are fresh, well, apart from my sleeping in them last night, assuming you don't mind. I have a sleeping bag and a collapsible camp bed I can kip on out here.'

'No, it's your place; I'm not pinching your bed; I'll have the camp bed.'

'Honestly, it's fine. Anyway, I prefer it out here; I can work when I get the urge, and I'll have this whisky with me to keep me company.'

'And there's me thinking we could share it.' We smile again at each other, looking into each other's eyes for probably a little longer than we should have.

I relent, 'OK, I'll put my bags in the bedroom if you're sure?'

'Absolutely, it's not a problem,' he replies, adding, 'the nights can still get a little chilly, so I'll light the log burner in there as well. Are you hungry yet?'

'I am, actually; I've not eaten much today.'

'Right then, I'll just grab some of my stuff from the bedroom, and while you unpack, I'll rustle us up something to eat.'

'Great, thank you.'

'The shower is pretty basic if you want to… there's plenty of hot water… when it's working, that is.'

'Ah yeah, I might, unless you want some help preparing dinner?'

'No, I'm good, thank you. Nothing special, but it'll be tasty and filling.'

'Looking forward to it.' Turning for the bedroom, I pull myself up, "*Looking forward to it*", what kind of thing to say is that?

We came up here a few years ago when Martin first bought this as a redundant building. He's spent some time and money doing it up to make it habitable. The bedroom is basic; all the walls in the building are random stone with lime mortar joints and whitewash paint. The roof is timber-framed, holding up a double-pitched slate roof, lined internally with pine boards, and the floors are the same large stone slabs throughout, not exactly built or designed for comfort. Heating is from the two log burners and the stove, and there is electricity from an overland cable to a local transformer. His place.

His retreat. I kind of like the feel of it; it has an old-world charm, straightforward and honest.

I don't really unpack, basically, because there is very little in the way of usable storage, just a small bedside cabinet with a drawer and a lower shelf, and a couple of wall shelves. There is a large hook on one wall acting as a coat hook with a couple of empty clothes hangers.

Taking my toiletries bag, I re-enter the living area and see Martin at the stove preparing dinner. He looks over his shoulder at me and smiles. 'Twenty to thirty minutes max,' he informs me.

'OK, great. I'll take that shower.'

'Sure. It's a simple electric shower. Turn it on, wait a couple of minutes, and it should get hot enough. Just turn the dial if you want more heat. I've put a couple of towels in there for you.'

'Thank you.'

Closing the wooden door behind me, there is no lock as such, just the lift latch. The shower is in one corner over a bathtub with a wraparound curtain. This really is basic stuff; I'm not sure what score I'll give it on TripAdvisor. Ah well, here goes.

34

Martin – The Bothy

I didn't anticipate her turning up, but she is welcome; in fact, I'm glad she's here. This will give us an opportunity to talk about everything that has gone on before and how we want to take our future forward together as friends or maybe something else; recently, I've been hoping it'll be the latter.

Melissa is out of the shower now, and I approach the bathroom door. I can hear her humming a tune to herself, which stops when I knock on the door. 'Hello, dinner will be ready in about five minutes.'

'Oh, OK, great, I'll be right out,' she replies.

Returning to the stove, I take the pan of meatballs and sauce off the hotplate, cover it with a lid, and place the pasta into the boiling water. As it simmers, I look into the water, drifting off in thoughts of what could be between the two of us. The bathroom door opens, and Melissa comes out; I turn to look at her, radiating a smile and warmth.

'Actually, that wasn't a bad shower. When I saw the curtain, I had visions of the movie Psycho,' she says through her smile.

'Haha, I never thought of it like that before.'

'So, Chef, what do we have for dinner this evening?'

'My signature dish, well, it is when I'm up here. Meatballs and tagliatelle, dressed with shavings of Parmigiano and black pepper, rustic bread drizzled with garlic, olive oil, and mixed herbs, accompanied by a bottle of Pinot Grigio.'

'Very nice, it smells delicious.'

'Well then, let's eat.'

We sit at the small table, now devoid of my laptop and latest book notes, replaced with food, wine, and a couple of lit candles. The log burner provides additional light as well as heat. In the distance, outside, there is the odd animal cry from the woods now and again and the distinctive sound of a barn owl. The logs crackle quietly, flickering patterns around the room.

Looking at her, the light catches her perfectly, and I want to kiss her, but I decide to take this slowly. 'Please, tuck in,' is the best I can muster; I don't want to rush anything and spoil the possibility of us becoming more than just good friends.

'Thank you. It looks great.'

'I only hope it tastes as good as it looks.'

'I'm sure it will.' She picks up the two forks in the pasta bowl and lifts a serving to her plate. Using a large spoon, I scoop up a couple of meatballs with sauce and place them on top of her pasta, and with the spoon, I point to the crusty bread beside the dish, 'It's the best I can do for garlic bread, Martino's Rustico,' kissing my fingers as I pull them from my lips; and I cringe a little after doing it.

'Thank you, Martino, very resourceful.'

I load my plate and pick up a slice of bread, dipping it in the sauce. Lifting it to my mouth, and before biting, I clumsily try to make small talk, 'You did well to remember how to get here and find my old Bothy.' I don't know why I'm feeling nervous; we've known each other for years.

'Yes, I drove up last time with Cr… Craig.' She pauses briefly, 'Once I have driven somewhere, I tend to more or less remember the journey from what I've noticed.' Looking at her, she is playing a little with her pasta; her mind is undoubtedly wandering at her mention of Craig. I need to engage her in something else.

'So, what do you think of my little writing retreat? I suppose it's missing a hot tub and barbeque.'

She looks up at me, 'No, it's great, a little basic but comfortable. Thank heavens for the log burners for warmth; I suppose they are a real godsend in winter.'

'Yep, but they do struggle to keep the place warm. At times, I have to resort to putting more wood in the stove as well and wearing extra clothes, so it's not often I come up in the depths of winter or when there is a really bad weather forecast. If it's too cold, I can't type much anyway; my fingers start to slow down.'

'Oh, I suppose they do. At least you have installed grid electricity.'

'Ah, well, yes, but unfortunately, the electricity supply is not that reliable; we often suffer brownouts up here, end of the line and all that. That's when the log burners and battery lamps come into their own.'

'Brownouts?'

'Reduction or loss of electricity supply. I have a small petrol generator just in case, but that only gives me limited power.'

'So, why do you like it here so much?'

'Because it's my place. I love the fresh air and solitude; the walks and scenery help clear my mind, allowing me to write without interruption or distraction.'

'Oh, I'm sorry, my being here won't help with that.'

'No, no, don't be silly, I love you being here, I'm glad you came up. Feel free to stay as long as you like.'

We eat and drink the wine, listen to the peace and quiet, and enjoy our time together just by being in each other's company. I keep stealing a look at her. I've never really noticed her before, not in the sense of wanting her. Maybe the deaths of Tanya and Craig have some benefit after all; it's allowed us the opportunity to find each other, to feel the attraction, when previously we didn't, or wouldn't, as we each had our spouses and respected the vows we had taken; unlike Tanya and Craig.

Finishing our food, Melissa makes to tidy away the dishes, and I intervene, 'It's fine, leave them, I'll clear up; you're my guest.'

'Nonsense, I'm the uninvited visitor.'

'No, please leave everything,' reaching for the wine bottle, 'A little more?'

'Yes, please.'

As I tip wine into her glass, Melissa, watching the wine pour, asks, 'Do you have internet access up here?'

'It's very limited. Why do you ask?'

'I was wondering about research for your writing, you know, if you needed to look up something.'

'I plan ahead, bringing with me what I think I'll need. If there is something I've forgotten that can't wait until I return to civilisation, I have to walk or drive until I can pick up a signal, then search for it on my laptop tethered to my mobile phone; and believe me, it can take some time due to the low-quality signal and low connection speed.'

'Wow, I hadn't realised how remote it is out here.'

'Another reason to think twice before coming up here in winter. So, what about you? What have you been up to?'

'Well, I returned to work last week. The Practice have been very good with me, patient and supportive, but it was time I tried to return to some normality. So, getting ready and returning to work has occupied my time recently, and before that, well, I suppose, sorting out the mess after everything that has happened. I always thought Craig was very organised, but I've since found out he was totally disorganised in his personal affairs. Luckily, we did draw up our Wills when he made Partner, although I think it was more his law firm that asked him to do it rather than him thinking about us. What about you?'

'I suppose I've been hiding in my writing after I got my head around the police investigation, the trial, and everything. I've been up here a couple of times, which has helped. When I returned to it, my writing did get a bit dark and heavy, though, and I think it spooked my Editor a little; that said, I'm coming out of that now with her guidance.'

'Good, I'm glad. Writing has always been your passion.'

'Yes, well, I did have that bad patch some time ago, and that is where good friends and Tanya's support helped.' As I say her name, I madden inside; the conflict of Tanya helping me one minute whilst sleeping with Craig the next. I don't know if Melissa can sense this torment inside me. Lifting the wine bottle, I pour some more into her glass and tip the remainder into mine. Placing it back on the table, keeping my hand on the bottle, I decide to share a thought with her.

'It's weird this, but I have this recurring thought running through my head; we normally drink a lot more than we did that weekend, but the two of us felt the effects far quicker than before, and our going to bed early saved our lives. The police said our wine was drugged with sleeping pills and...' As I say it, I notice she stops nibbling at the bread in her hand, holding it still at her lips. A worried expression spreads over her face, as though I had said something sensitive or more like insensitive; I remind myself again that I need to stop talking at times and just stick to writing. She picks up the wine glass and then, just as quickly, places it back down again, turning the stem of the glass between her thumb and forefinger, looking into the wine as though it holds some cryptic message.

'I feel tired. Do you mind if we call it a night? It was a long drive up here, and I need to dry my hair before bed.'

'Er, no, not at all.' Worried I said something offensive, I grasp the nettle, 'Sorry, did I say something wrong?'

'No, it's just me, I'm tired.' She stands, pushing the chair back slightly, and turning to step away from the table. She uses the back of the chair to hold her steady, causing the chair to rock slightly on the uneven floor, and she overcompensates in her reaction, as though she has drunk too much. 'I'm going to bed now. Goodnight, Martin.'

I push my chair back, and before I am fully standing, she is already making her way to the bedroom. I call out behind her, 'Would you like some water?'

She stops, taking in and letting out a deep breath, her shoulders rising and falling, but not looking at me. 'Yes, please. That'll be good, I think. Thank you.'

I take a small bottle of water from the kitchen worktop and pass it to her, adding, 'It can get chilly at night up here; feel free to put more logs in the burner in your room if you want to.'

'Thank you, Martin.' She turns to look at me. 'I enjoyed dinner,' then turns away and continues to the bedroom, closing the door behind her.

What just happened? We were getting on great, and then, bang. It's like that time at the church.

Clearing the table and putting the plates beside the sink, I decide to leave them there until morning. Taking the bottle of single malt and my favourite whisky glass from the small cupboard over the sink, I wander to my settee and drop down into the comfort of the old, worn leather. Removing the seal and twisting the cork stopper from the bottle, I gently pour a good measure of whisky. Placing the bottle on the floor beside me, I lift the glass and look at the log burner flames through the amber spirit, slowly twirling the contents before placing it beneath my nostrils. Savouring the moment, a small bang from the bedroom distracts me, but there is no further noise. I sip the whisky and let it linger before swallowing.

What did I say? I mentioned what the police said about the wine, and that seems to have flicked a switch in her; was that the trigger that changed the mood? Did that really happen, or am I being a little paranoid, and she is just tired? I'm probably reading too much into this. I'll see if I can bring it up again tomorrow if I find the right moment.

I must admit, I'm getting tired now. I'm not sure what time it is, as I never wear a watch up here and won't have a clock in the place. It must be late. I drink the last of the whisky in my glass and close my eyes for a minute, thinking.

35

Melissa – The Bothy

Why did he mention that? That freaked me out. It shouldn't have done; I thought I had all that behind me and locked away. I was getting too comfortable with him, I think, enjoying the moment, and then it just brought me back down to earth with a bump.

It is a little chilly now, and as I look at the burner, the flame is low. Putting on the protective glove, I open the burner door, place another seasoned log on the one already flickering, and close the door. Opening the vent a little, the extra oxygen feeds the flames, which start to wrap around the new log. Within a minute or so, the log has caught, and I slide the vent back.

I don't want to go back through the living room to the bathroom just yet; Martin may try to restart the conversation. Deciding to wait until he's fallen asleep, I undress beside the fire, pull on some warm pyjamas, then kneel before the fire, lowering my head in front of the hot glass, and start to run my fingers through my damp hair to dry it. I can hear him quietly moving around in the living room, and the small pop of the cork is him probably opening the whisky. It's all quiet now.

Feeding my hair through my fingers helps to calm me down, reminding me of my mum slowly brushing my hair when I was young; she would often hum or softly sing along to a tune on the radio or, on occasion, talk about holidays or planning for a family event. I'm missing my mum; I wish she were here now, but then I can't tell her what I did; she would be horrified that her beautiful little girl could do such a thing. A small tear forms in the corner of my eye, and I wipe it on the back of my pyjama sleeve.

My hair is practically dry now, but I'm starting to feel the cold stone floor, which is not the best to sit on. Moving away from the fire, I feel the room's chill, so I return and place another smaller log in the burner to help provide a heat boost, clunking the door shut and adjusting the vent slightly. I climb into bed and put my head on the pillow, twisting to turn off the small bedside lamp. Looking up at the ceiling, I watch the melody of soft flame light dance across the wooden boards and listen to the crackle of the fire, joined in chorus with the distant forest sounds outside. I slowly close my eyes.

Craig, Martin, and Tanya are laughing in a pub, followed by images of us walking across fields to a cottage in the woods; we're all happy, having fun, but as I open the door to the cottage, a giant demonic face, ablaze with fire and raw rage jumps up in front of me. I scream, but I'm unable to make any sound. With a startle, I snap out of my nightmare, sitting bolt upright in bed, panting heavily, hot, and clammy. I thought I'd left my night terrors behind me some time ago, but something has triggered them again. The fire is low, and the light dim, and as I reach for the lamp and flick the switch, the cold air hits my skin and makes me shiver. Opening the top drawer, I remove my little zip pouch, open it, and look for my sleeping pills. Twisting the cap off the water bottle, I swallow two tablets, throwing my head back as I take them down. I recall Tanya telling me something about Martin's depression and his difficulty getting to sleep, but he came out of that episode only to end up in this one. I wonder how he's coping.

Leaving the bedside lamp on and lying back down, drilling myself deeper under the duvet, I curl up to get warmer. I wish Martin were here beside me now. I could snuggle up to him and feel safe, warm, and protected. We'll have a good chat tomorrow, air how we feel about each other and find out if we have a future together or not.

36

Melissa – The Bothy

Thursday, 25th April

It's the low noises from the living area that start to wake me, and I'm surprised it's already light when I reach for my watch beside the bed; ten seventeen a.m., I'm startled I slept for as long as I did, I must have been more tired than I thought I was, or I suppose it could have been the pills I'd taken. I'd fallen asleep with the side lamp on and hadn't noticed, obviously needing the extra sleep to recharge my batteries. I switch off the lamp, swing my legs out of bed, and feel a slight chill in the room. Looking at the log burner, it's clear from the ashes that it went cold hours ago.

I change into my jeans, pull on a T-shirt and sweat top and doing so, I feel a little unsteady standing and have a slight headache. It can't be the wine; we only shared a bottle. I hope I'm not coming down with something. Pulling the window curtains aside, the glass has a layer of condensed water droplets on the inside, so I open the side pane slightly to let in some air and help clear the condensation. The air is crisp and fresh, and over the distant hills, I can see dark clouds; breathing in deeply helps me come around. I notice a deer nibbling vegetation about thirty metres away at the edge of the wood on the far side of the track; wow, it is so peaceful here.

As I open the door to the living area, Martin is sitting at the table typing quickly on his laptop, engrossed in the screen. I move to cross the floor, and he pauses, turns his head, looks up at me, and greets me with a smile: 'Good morning. Did you sleep well?'

'Good morning, I think I did. Or should I say, good afternoon?'

'Haha, see, that's what I like about this place: the tranquillity; it's so easy to lose track of time. You obviously needed a long sleep. Do you fancy a coffee? I'll rustle us up with a cooked breakfast for brunch if you like.'

'Coffee will be good, yes, please. But I'm not so sure about a cooked breakfast. Maybe just some plain toast?' I reply, rubbing my eyes, still feeling a little groggy.

'Are you OK? You look a bit peaky.'

'Yeh, I'm fine, just still a little tired.' Looking down at his laptop, 'Are you writing?'

As he rises from the table, he replies, 'Yes, I woke early, so thought I'd make the most of the time while you slept; I feel invigorated, so thought I'd put it to good use. I didn't wake you, did I?'

'No, no, not at all,' I reply with a little white lie.

'OK, great. I thought I would go for a long walk this morning; rain is forecast to hit late this afternoon. Do you fancy tagging along?'

'Yes, that'll be good, but I don't have any walking gear with me.'

'Don't worry, Tan…' he pauses for a second, 'I have some spare boots and a walking coat you can try on. I'll get that coffee and toast.'

'Thank you.' I enter the bathroom and close the door behind me.

How do I feel about wearing clothes that clearly belonged to a dead woman, Tanya? Don't be silly; they're just clothes; there is no mystique about them. I wash, and as I didn't do it last night, I brush my teeth with extra special attention this morning.

Back in the living area, Martin has poured coffee, and two slices of toast are on a plate beside the coffee cup. He is standing, leaning against the kitchen worktop, with his hands wrapped around a cup. Approaching the table, I look around for the collapsible camp bed, but I can't see one. 'I hope you slept well in here last night; you do have a camp bed, don't you?'

'Yes, I do, but, well, actually, I fell asleep on the settee, bad habit when I take a nightcap and have the log fire going,' he nods his head in the direction of the whisky bottle near the sink.

'Sorry, I feel awful, pinching your bedroom.'

'It's fine, not a problem. Now I'll get that gear together while you have your coffee and toast.'

Martin takes a big drink of his coffee and places his cup down before leaving by the front door. I notice him walk down the side of the Bothy, crossing one of the small gable end windows. I walk up to the window and watch him unlock a small timber shed I hadn't noticed before, and after a minute or so, he emerges with boots in his left hand and a red walker's coat over his arm. When he returns, I am sitting down again beside his laptop, nibbling my toast.

'Another crime thriller? Are you carrying on with the series?'

'No, something a little different, something I have been playing around with in my head for some time.'

'Great, looking forward to reading it.'

'It'll be a couple of months yet before it's in a presentable state.' He places the boots on the floor and the coat over the arm of the settee. 'Here we go. If the boots are a bit too big, I have some spare socks, which may help.'

'Thank you.'

He walks into the bedroom and returns a few minutes later wearing green cargo-type walking trousers and a red lumberjack check shirt over a white T-shirt. 'Right, ready when you are,' he smiles at me, warm and pleasant. He doesn't seem to be holding a grudge because I went to bed early last night; it looks like I'm forgiven.

37

Martin – The Moors

Out on the moorland, walking between pine forest plantations has given us the opportunity to catch up with each other, the latest with family and friends. We try to stay clear of the murders and the aftermath, and the trial collapsing, well, not collapsing as such, but stopping in the way it did. It's good to talk with someone who has been through it with you, who understands and appreciates the pain and frustration, the anger, and the upset, but not have the need to talk about it just because, well, we know it and it is still quite raw for us both.

The clouds are rolling in lower now, darker, and across the valley; we can see the rain falling like a misty screen onto the moors in the distance. We are heading back towards the Bothy, but we could get caught out here if we're not careful.

'I think we'd better pick up our pace now,' I say to Melissa, pointing at the weather front, 'it's coming in a little quicker than I expected.'

'Yes, it does look menacing.'

'We can cut the corner across here if you don't mind a little mud and a beck crossing? We might get our feet a bit wet.'

'No, that's fine. Let's do it.'

We climb a stile over a fence line, allowing us to enter one of the plantations. The trees are rustling in the light wind, and it's quite dark amongst them. As she steps down, I hold out my hand, and she takes it. Looking around, she asks, 'Is it OK to cut through here? We're not trespassing, are we?'

'No, it's fine. This is a designated pathway. Down this hillside, cross the beck, then up the other side, and we'll be almost on top of the Bothy when we break out of the trees.'

'OK, lead the way.'

I stride out, breaking a faster pace, and Melissa keeps up with me. Within five minutes, we are at the beck, a swiftly flowing peat brown water running over a rocky bottom with odd boulders dotted about, creating small eddies and broken water.

I turn to Melissa. 'The bank is steep, and the grass is slippery. The rocks in the beck are too. Be careful where you stand and steady with each footing before committing.'

'It doesn't look that bad,' she replies.

'Believe me, it's slippery. I'll go in first; you follow, and then I help you up on the other side.'

'OK.'

I dig my feet into the wet grass, making sure I have a decent purchase before putting my weight on each footstep. Entering the beck, the water comes over the top of my boots, and instantly, I feel the icy cold hit my feet. Standing, I turn to Melissa and hold out my right arm, beckoning her to come forward. She moves forward slowly, sensibly, copying me, digging in her boots to the grassy bank. As her left foot enters the water, she puts her weight forward and instantly screams, 'Bloody hell, that's cold!' and I laugh. 'You didn't say it was going to be that cold.'

'If I had done, you might not have done it. Come on, nearly there,' I grab her hand firmly and tease her forward. She puts her right foot onto a rock, trying to keep it out of the water and before I could say no, she puts her weight onto her right leg and moves forward.

Her foot slips off the rock and lands in the water, and she stumbles on the uneven, rocky bottom. I lunge forward to catch her and pull her in close to me.

In my arms, she looks up at me, 'Thank you. You are my saviour.'

'I did say it would be slippery.'

'I know, but now you have me trapped in your arms, standing in a freezing cold beck. What do we do next?'

It just happened. I lower my head and kiss her, and in doing so, she kisses me right back. In the moment, I couldn't feel the cold water numbing my feet or the sky getting darker above us. We kiss more, our embrace getting tighter. This moment is special; it wasn't planned; it simply happened: two people in the middle of nowhere, finding each other at long last.

It is the rain that rudely interrupts us, turning from nothing to a deluge. It startles us both, and we pull back from each other. Looking into each other's eyes, we start laughing.

'Come on, let's get back to the Bothy before we drown.'

She laughs some more, and I turn to the opposite grassy bank and dig in my boots. Turning, I hold my hand out, and she grabs it, bouncing past me with an agility I didn't expect, straight up the bank and to the top. 'Come on, slowcoach,' she teases. And with that, I don't need any further encouragement.

We run back to the Bothy in the heavy rain and rush in through the front door, dripping wet. Pulling my rain hood back, I speak loudly over the rustling wet clothes and the rain hitting the slate roof: 'Leave your boots and wet clothes here, and I'll sort them out. You had best grab a warm shower, and I'll get the fires lit.'

'OK.'

Melissa starts to shake a little now, realising the cold water she is drenched with. She peels off her wet coat and bends to unfasten the laces to her boots, kicking them off to one side behind the door. She pulls off her wet socks and then slowly peels down her wet trousers, pulling the right leg over her naked foot. I wasn't expecting her to strip in front of me, and she senses it, cocking her head to one side, looking at me with a smile. 'Now, don't be getting any ideas, well, not just yet', she teases.

I know I'm blushing slightly, and she sees it, softly giggling as she stands upright, planting another kiss on my lips before running for the bathroom. I know I have an enormous grin across my face, bigger than a Cheshire Cat's.

Taking off my coat and picking up Melissa's, I hang them on the back of the door, the drips forming small pools on the flagstone floor. I pull off my boots, and as I walk to the log burner, I leave a trail of wet footprints on the cold floor. Opening the door, I put a match to the fire I'd laid earlier, and it ignites easily. The paper and kindling taking rapidly, with the logs attracting the flames. I cross to the stove, and it's still warm; I re-stock it with logs, which also quickly take.

Reaching for the whisky bottle, I pour us two glasses, swallow mine down and refill it. The warmth is welcoming, although not much good for my cold feet. I pull off my wet trousers and socks and put all the wet clothes in a pile beside the burner. I'll get the drying stand out after I get myself dry first.

The shower is running, and Melissa is humming away to herself. I wander around the room, closing window curtains and sliding the bolt across the front door. Entering the bedroom, I re-set the logs with kindling and old newspaper and ignite the fire with matches. It takes quickly, and I close the door and adjust the vent to get a steady burn.

As I stand and step back, Melissa enters the bedroom wrapped in a large towel with a smaller towel around her head, holding her damp hair.

'Ooo, lovely, thank you.' She walks up to me and gives me a short kiss whilst leaning into me. 'Your turn for a shower; your feet are almost blue.'

I look down at them, and they are. 'Yep, hope you've left me some hot water?'

'Hope so.' She smiles in reply.

'There is a tot of whisky on the table for you. It will help warm you through. I'll be out shortly.'

38

Melissa – The Bothy

This is wonderful. I was hoping this would happen, and it's happened naturally; not forced, not planned, not contrived. I think he feels it, too, that we are good for each other and that we can be happy together. I know, slowly, slowly, we mustn't rush into this. We both need to be sure this is what we want.

We already have a friendship that we can build on, a shared grief that unites us, and a mutual attraction that can easily develop. I never thought through all those years of being two couples in a friendship could lead us to this, to the two of us being together. This is the good that came out of that weekend; I couldn't have predicted my actions leading up to that weekend would bring us together as naturally as this, but I'm glad I did what I did now. Wow, that's the first time I've thought like that. Martin was shocked when he found out about their affair like I was, but I knew before that weekend. Martin only became aware of their relationship after they were murdered. How dare Craig think he can have his sordid way with my friend, the wife of my other friend. Craig held no respect for other people's feelings; it was always what he wanted when he wanted it, and invariably on his terms. Did I know it would end up like this? No. Did I hope it would? Well, maybe, yes. But I didn't expect them to be murdered, effectively clearing the path for us to be together. That, as it has turned out, is a bonus.

I sip at the whisky Martin poured, standing by the fire in the bedroom, warming me inside and out. I can hear him in the bathroom next door; he's humming like I do when I shower. We were meant to be together.

He's turned off the shower. Now that the running water has stopped, I can hear him clearer; he sounds happy.

Wandering back into the living area, the room is warmer now, the log burner with the stove's contribution taking effect. I should see what food we have available and see if there is something I can prepare quickly. Opening the small fridge, there is not a great deal inside: a packet of butter, milk, some eggs and bacon, some beer and a couple of bottles of wine, a typical man-stocked fridge that contrasts with the avocado, olives, and the Greek yoghurt I brought up with me. In the cupboard above the sink, there are a few tins of food, and eventually, I decide on a large tin of Scottish Beef Broth and some buttered crusty bread I could warm through in the oven. Simple and hearty.

Martin comes out of the bathroom to find me at the stove, stirring the pan of broth. He approaches me, puts his arms around my waist, and peeps over my shoulder.

'Umm, smells good.'

'Thank you. And what about the soup?'

He laughs and squeezes me in his arms, then whispers, 'Would you like another tot of whisky?'

'No thanks, but I can see why it is your favourite. I'll have some wine, though.'

'No problem.' Martin takes a bottle of wine from the fridge and extracts the cork. 'Shall I let it breathe or…?'

'No,' giggling, 'it's fine, you know me, pour away,' smiling at him.

With the poor weather, darkness crawls in earlier this evening. The closed curtains, the log fires, the warm food, and the drinks will all work, hopefully, to make this a very special evening.

Sitting at the small table opposite each other, we chat and laugh about anything that comes to mind: holidays, funny events, school days, nicknames, favourite movies, and music, and before we know it, the bottle of wine is empty, and Martin is removing the cork from a second bottle.

'At this rate, we'll need to drive into a town to restock sooner rather than later,' I jokingly say to him as he takes a drink of his wine.

'That's rich, coming from you.' His reply is a bit cutting.

'Sorry?'

'Saying I've got a drink problem when it's you who has the problem.'

I don't know what set this off. 'I beg your pardon?'

'Tyler on the Tiles, they used to call you.'

His expression is odd; the venom in his manner has just come from nowhere. What happened? What did I say?

'Sorry, Martin, did I say something wrong?'

'Well, it won't be the first time, will it?

I can't believe how fast his mood has changed. Is he playing with me? If he is, I'm not enjoying the joke. Looking at him, I don't think he's joking.

'Martin, that's not very nice; why would you say that?'

'Forget it,' as he looks down at the table.

'No. What do you mean by that?'

'You keep bringing up Craig and Tanya.'

'No, I don't. I mentioned them, yes, but we were talking about holidays together. They were with us; you remember that, don't you?'

In a raised voice, slamming his wine glass on the table, 'Oh, now I have a bad memory as well, do I?'

His sudden change and raised voice are scaring me, and without thinking, I turn it back on him, 'Well, yes, maybe you do have a drinking problem. If you hadn't drunk that much on that night, maybe they would still both be with us!' I can't believe I just said that to him, and as I finish, he throws the wine glass across the room to smash on the floor in the far corner.

'Fuck off! You can't blame me for what happened.'

Now I am scared. I didn't know he had such mood swings; my blood is boiling now. I start shouting at him, not sure what I'm saying, and he shouts back at me. He's slamming his hands on the table, making the bowls and cutlery rattle. My hands are shaking; I'm unsure if it's anger or fright. He's pacing the room, throwing his arms around; do I continue to fight or take flight? I want to fight it out but decide on the latter, taking, I hope, the safest option. I push the chair back, and the back legs catch on the stone floor. As I stand, the chair falls backwards, clattering on the stone flags. He spins around to look at me; I hold my hands and pace backwards towards the bedroom.

'That's it. Just like her, duck out when the going gets tough. You women are all the same; why would I think you would be any different?'

'Martin! Enough! I don't want to fight; I'm going to my room.'

'That's my room, I think you'll find!'

I turn quickly and run for the bedroom door as I'm not sure what he'll do, and I slam the door behind me. The only thing I can use to lock the door is a wooden chair, and I push the back of it under the timber cross beam of the door, wedging it tight. Backing away from the door, I hear him mumbling something, but I can't make out what he's saying. A few minutes pass, and everything is quiet. As my adrenalin starts to subside and my shaking slows down, I begin feeling the chill in the room. Bending down to the fire, I open the door and throw in a log that hits the back of the burner and dislodges the burning logs already in there. I pull the vent wide open, and the log catches fast. I turn to the bed. I climb under the duvet, fully dressed, and pull it up over me, pulling my legs up to my chest, keeping my gaze firmly on the door. Running things over in my mind, I can't recall the trigger that set him off; he mentioned I kept talking about Tanya and Craig, and maybe it is all still too raw for him; he hasn't come to terms with what happened. This has me worrying again about my part in all this; the torment in my head starts to reawaken. After about twenty to twenty-five minutes, I hear Martin snoring; he must have fallen asleep on the settee. I'm also tired, and my eyes start to close, and soon, I slip into a deep sleep.

39

Martin – The Bothy

Friday, 26th April

I wake unsure of the time, and my head is swirling like a wind turbine in a hurricane; I'm still tired, my back aches badly, and my legs feel heavy as I plant them on the floor. That was a bad night's sleep. Putting my head in my hands with elbows on my knees, it starts coming back to me; shit, we argued, and I lost it with her. Oh my god, what happened; what did I do? Did I cause it?

Raising my head, trying to focus through the nausea, I look about the room and see a broken glass in the corner, dinner bowls and mess on the table, but no sign of Melissa. The bedroom door is closed, but I can't hear anything. I stand and nearly fall over; my legs are weak or not working properly; how much did I drink? I look around and find the bottle of whisky almost empty, lying on its side with the cork stopper missing. Carefully, using the tabletop for support, I wander to the window beside the stone fireplace and pull back the curtains, and daylight blinds me, making me close my eyes quickly in an attempt to evade the laser beams searing into my eye sockets. Slowly regaining my vision and fighting back the urge to be sick, I risk opening my eyes slowly and see both cars are still outside, which is a relief; at least she is still here.

Stepping carefully around the broken glass, I remove a broom and brush pan from the utility cupboard and start to slowly sweep up the shards when I hear a slight clattering at the bedroom door and the latch lifting.

Remaining slightly bent over, working on this most essential task, I'm doing a terrible job of trying to avoid eye contact with Melissa as she leaves the bedroom. Out of the corner of my eye, I see her quietly but swiftly, walking to the bathroom and closing the door behind her. For a small Bothy, there is a very large elephant in the room now. What did I say? I can't believe I lost my temper with Melissa; she has been so good, so kind, and so understanding, especially considering all the things we've both been through.

Tipping the broken glass into the plastic refuse bin beside the sink, I stow away the brush and pan, turn to the stove, and open the door to insert some logs. Looking inside, the embers are low, and it takes some stoking and more paper and kindling to get it going again, but it starts to burn. I fill the kettle and place it on the hot plate, knowing it'll take some time to heat up. The toilet flushes and Melissa runs the water in the sink to wash, then brushes her teeth. I'm clearing the table when she opens the bathroom door and slowly walks out into the living area; I decide to go straight to the nettle and grasp it.

'Melissa. I think I owe you an apology. I don't know what came over me last night. I'm so sorry. I didn't mean to say what I did or lose my temper, especially not with you.' As I'm speaking, I feel the nausea rising in me. I must look rough.

'Are you OK, Martin? I mean, you look awful.'

'It's my own fault, the aftereffects of excessive self-inflicted spirits. Look, I'm really sorry; I hope you can forgive me?'

'Shall we just tidy up and get some breakfast? We can talk about it later. I need some time to think.'

'Sure, so long as we do talk, I feel awful about last night.'

'Let's have some breakfast. I'm sure it'll do you good. Then maybe we can go for a long walk, escape these walls for a bit, and get a bit of nature. Can we do that?'

'Yes, thank you.'

I wander into the bathroom and turn the shower on; the sound of the water hitting the bath and the shower curtain makes my head hurt, but I need to do this. Slowly stripping while trying to stop myself from falling over is a challenge, but I get there and step over the bath side into the shower. The cool water hits my head like a thousand hailstones, and the shock forces me to pull my head from the water for a few seconds before I plunge it back into the maelstrom. Within a few minutes, I start to come around and feel more awake, more with it. I need to cut back on the drinking. I hadn't realised it, but it's affecting me and my moods.

Entering the living area, Melissa has placed a pot of coffee, a large glass of water, and some toast on the now-clear table. She's pulled all the curtains, and the front door is open, letting in additional light and fresh air. I can now hear the birds outside in the trees and feel the presence of nature enveloping us.

'Come on, sit down, have something to eat and drink; there are a couple of paracetamol tablets on your plate, all part of a well-balanced diet for a morning like this.'

I look at her, and she has a light smile on her face, maybe a little forced; I can't tell, but she is trying to make me feel better about the situation. She's thought of all my immediate needs, and I feel lousy for being such a bad friend.

'Thank you, Melissa, you didn't need to; I don't deserve this,' I say a little sheepishly, taking a seat. She joins me and pours two cups of coffee while I wash the pills down with water.

'I thought we could go for a long walk and maybe find a pub for lunch if there's one around here. Sound good?' she asks.

'Yes, it does, but I think I'll stay away from the beer,' looking back at her with a repentant schoolboy grin.

'Hair of the dog is more likely the order of the day, I think,' she titters slightly before sipping her coffee.

40

Melissa – Kielder Forest

It really is beautiful up here. Walking through pine forests along logging roads, now and again breaking through trees on vistas across fields, hills, and Kielder Water. We've been walking for about two and half hours now, passing the odd hillwalker or couple heading in different directions, acknowledging each other, but other than that, it's peaceful and remote. The long silences are growing shorter now, and we are talking about our surroundings, Martin sharing stories of him doing up the Bothy, once turning up to find two walkers asleep in his bed thinking it was a public Bothy, turning a spin on Goldie Locks making me laugh. This is the Martin I know.

Martin directs us to a small pub in a village of maybe no more than ten or twelve cottages, and we enjoy a nice Ploughman's lunch, a pint of real ale for Martin and a glass of wine for me: a very pleasant day all round considering last night's fireworks. We've not really talked of last night; I suppose we're both afraid we may re-ignite something that neither of us wants to. It's probably for the best.

By the time we return to the Bothy, its late afternoon, and the sun is bearing down on the hills to the west. It's been an enjoyable walk, and for the last mile or so, we've been holding hands and appreciating this time with each other.

The wave of guilt that came over me again last night when we argued has all but disappeared, but I know it's still there, not far from the surface but sufficiently contained to allow me to laugh again. Martin is back to his usual jovial self, talking about doing some writing before dinner this evening. He maintains these walks fuel his creative side, managing to clear away life's usual troubles and worries, letting his imaginative streak come forward and play with ideas and storylines.

Sure enough, no sooner are we inside the Bothy than he sits at the table with his laptop open, typing away with a passion; it's great to see him back on form.

I spend the next couple of hours cleaning out the log fires and kitchen area, not that it is my job or expected of me, but they need doing, and Martin is so engrossed in his work. I've laid and set the fires, and as darkness falls, I prepare our dinner; nothing fancy, game pie we bought today from the pub, along with some potatoes I've mashed, green runner beans and a small pot of gravy.

Turning the room lights on interrupts Martin, and he sits back from his keyboard, his first break in nearly two hours.

'Sorry, I didn't mean to disturb you; it's just that it's getting dark, and dinner is almost ready.'

'No, it's fine; I need a break. Wow, that was fantastic; I had been struggling with that scene in my head for weeks, trying to make it work, and I've cracked it now,' he says, looking at me as though it's the first time he's seen me in years; the joy on his face is heavenly, I could lose myself in this moment. We look at each other, smiling, not speaking. He stands, walks to me, and as his arms wrap around me, our lips meet, and we kiss deeply, the passion of his writing transferring through his lips, his hands, to my back, my neck, my face, passion running through me. I kiss him, fully receptive to him, our bodies moving slowly in time, getting closer, tighter together.

The kettle on the stove starts to whistle as it releases steam, bringing us back to our senses; as we pull our heads away from each other, I lower mine and place my cheek on his chest, snuggling him, closing my eyes, savouring the moment. The whistle gets louder, and Martin speaks first, 'Saved by the whistle. I'd better get that,' and he releases his embrace and steps towards the stove.

I suddenly feel lost, standing in the middle of the room alone. I spin on the spot and busy myself with the table setting as Martin returns to remove his laptop and notepad. Our hands touch when we both reach for his pen, and we look at each other, smiling, feeling like two youngsters catching a forbidden but knowing moment. I laugh, and he joins me.

Last night is a distant memory, feeling like it happened a long time ago to two different people. This is the Martin I know and love, the one I want to be with; mine.

As we eat, we talk and laugh again, look at each other and touch hands. We share a bottle of wine, just a couple of glasses each, being cautious about not drinking too much alcohol tonight. I feel like I need to monitor how much Martin drinks, and it's as though he is thinking the same thing, not initiating refilling our glasses.

A part of me wants to ask him what happened last night and what made him lose his temper with me, but another part is telling me to be sensible and not do it; it'll flare up again. We haven't really mentioned it, save for his apology this morning. Am I happy about leaving it there? If he still has deep issues with the murders, he'll be better talking about them, sharing the pain or anger so it can be addressed or treated if needs be. If he doesn't, it'll eat away at him, fester and blow up at the wrong moment like it did last night.

'Martin, do you think we could make it together?'

'How do you mean? In a relationship?'

'Well, yes. We are good together, aren't we?'

'Yes, I suppose we are. Is that what you want?' he cautiously questions.

'I think it is.' He looks at his empty bowl while playing with the spoon. I wasn't expecting his hesitation, so I continue, 'We are good friends and today we spent some enjoyable time together. We laugh and want the same things in life, don't you think?'

'Yes, I suppose. But…'

'But what?'

'We each have our ghosts to contend with,' he replies without lifting his head to look at me.

His tone has moved, more melancholy now. 'How do you mean, ghosts?' As soon as I ask the question, I regret it, risking him slipping back into a deeper mood.

'Tanya for me and Craig for you,' replying quietly.

'We can't let their deaths define how we now want to live our lives, Martin; we survived; we have to carry on.'

'But do you not think it's wrong that our future should be that we are together? After all, we never had these feelings for each other when they were alive.'

It is comforting to hear him use the words "*feelings for each other*", but he's clearly struggling more with this than I first thought.

'I'm not so sure about that, Martin; I sometimes thought there was a little more to our friendship than being just good friends. Did you not sense that, did you not feel it?'

'To be honest, no; there was only Tanya for me. She was my one, and I'm lost without her.'

He's still not yet come to terms with the fact that she has gone. Maybe I am pushing this too fast, and I need to slow down, or I could risk losing him altogether. I want to spend my life with Martin. Does he not appreciate what I've done for him?

'I wish I could say the same about Craig. I couldn't get my head around his persistent adultery with other women.'

'Well, maybe if you had brought his ways to a stop, he wouldn't have had an affair with my wife!'

He's flipped again; the aggression is evident in his raised tone and choice of words.

'You do know it takes two to tango, Martin. Tanya went along with it with him; she wasn't coerced into it.'

'What do you know about it? How can you know what happened? I know I was in a bad place, and I could have forgiven her for finding some comfort in the arms of another at that time.'

'Really!? Do you think so? Hindsight is twenty-twenty vision, Martin; you know that right!'

'Fuck off!' he shouts, throwing the bowl across the room into the small pile of logs by the fire, bouncing off and smashing on the stone floor, the spoon spinning across the slabs.

'Well, I know more than you know!'

'And what is that supposed to mean?'

I've said too much, and he repeats, 'Well, what is that supposed to mean?'

'Nothing! You're just getting me angry now!'

'Bollocks! You know something, don't you?'

This is getting out of hand again; one of us needs to stop to remove the fuel from this heated exchange, and I decide it's going to be me. Almost as a repeat of last night, I stand and walk quickly to the bedroom and shout out, 'Just leave it will you,' as I slam the bedroom door behind me.

Leaning against the door, I hear him continue kicking furniture and throwing things around; he is so wound up that any release is dangerous. The low light of the log burner gives enough illumination for me to cross the room and turn on the bedside lamp, and just like last night, I climb into bed and pull the duvet up around me, looking at the door, quietly hoping he won't come in; but then again, hoping he will. This is fiery and passionate. I need to find a way to control his temper so that we can talk and get to the root of the issues, allowing us to move forward together.

I hear Martin open the front door and slam it hard again; then, all is quiet.

What happened that night still haunts me, but obviously, something haunts him more. If I hadn't made the decision I made, I might have had a better chance at us being together as a couple now. But how could I have done it differently? The decisions I made, I still believe, are the best on the balance of probabilities, especially given the events as they unfolded and were presented to me; maybe he just has to see that for himself, to appreciate what I did was for his benefit as well; for our benefit.

It's quiet in the living room now. He must have gone for a walk or outside simply to calm down. I turn off the bedside lamp and lie down under the duvet, looking up at the ceiling, watching light and shadows dance overhead from the flames of the fire, that feeling of déjà vu sweeping over me.

I don't remember falling asleep and have no idea how long I've been sleeping, but the clanking noise of the door opening on the burner and seeing Martin bent low, feeding in another log, brings me around. He looks over his shoulder to me, 'I'm sorry, I didn't mean to wake you. The outside temperature has dropped tonight, and there's an arctic wind coming in from the east, I thought I'd better keep the fires going.' His voice and manner are calm, almost soothing.

Intent on keeping things calm, I reply softly, 'That's kind of you, Martin, thank you.'

He closes the door and walks around the bed. With his right hand indicating the empty bed space beside me, he asks, 'Do you mind?'

I wasn't expecting that. 'Er, erm, no.'

He sits on the edge of the bed, removes his boots, rotates, and then leans back, bringing his sock-covered feet up on top of the duvet. He shuffles up to a pillow behind him and props himself up against the head frame in a sitting-up position, crossing his hands in his lap. Into the semi-dark, he speaks quietly and softly, 'I'm sorry. It seems I'm apologising more and more these days, but I truly am sorry.'

41

Martin – the Bothy bedroom

'…I truly am.' I hope she believes my sincerity. My night walk through the forest has helped me clear my head and think rationally of how I feel about the situation, about Melissa, about us. I can see there being an "us", although I know I will have to wrestle with my demons and dispel them before we can find happiness together.

I feel her move under the duvet I've semi-pinned her under, sensing she is twisting slightly to look at me. I look down at her and see her face looking back up at me, partly illuminated by the warming flames.

'I know you are. I hope you realise I only want the best for us,' she replies.

'I do, and I promise to come to terms with my feelings. I know I need to move on, but it isn't easy. Tanya was the love of my life, and for her to be taken like that, doing what she was doing, I'm struggling with it.'

Her left arm emerges from beneath the duvet, and she places it across me softly, her palm on my chest. 'I know Martin, I know. Losing them both was a massive shock to us both, and I appreciate it being more so for you. I knew what Craig was like with other women, but I refused to confront it with him. You are right; maybe things would have ended differently if I had done.'

'But it would have ended, is that what you're saying?'

'Yes, I think I am. Yes, we would have eventually divorced, of that I'm sure, and I have come to realise that

I was living in denial, not wanting to believe he was treating me badly.'

I pull my left arm free from between us and place it over hers, drawing her closer, putting my hand over the back of hers, caressing her hand softly with my fingers, empathising with her, showing my affection and understanding. I'm enjoying this moment we have; her breathing is soft and light, barely audible over the crackling fire. Looking down at her, her head is against my chest, and her eyes are closed; if it can stay like this, I will be happy. I don't want to spoil this moment, and I bite my lip, refraining from saying something that could upset either of us; this will be a fragile relationship if this is the only way we can exist together. We both know we need to say something to each other, but the unspoken words come between us, neither daring to fracture the precarious peace we find in moments like this.

We lie holding each other for some time, listening to the wind blowing through the forest outside, generating a meditative atmosphere, gently and peacefully bringing nature into our room, our space. A log tumbles in the burner, bringing a splash of light and crackles. Melissa slowly draws her knees up under the duvet, snuggling me closer, adopting a curled-up-like foetal position. As I close my eyes, Melissa hits me with a bombshell, 'I put something in our wine that night to help us sleep.'

I stop gently caressing her hand and lie absolutely still, not knowing what to say next. After about twenty seconds, she quietly repeats her statement, 'Martin, did you hear me? I put something in our wine that night to help us sleep.'

'Yes, I heard you. Why would you do that?'

Without moving her position, she answers quietly, 'I'm struggling with my guilt of what I did that night. I laced the white wine with some crushed sleeping pills because I needed us both to be upstairs, away from them and away from the third bedroom, so that they had free reign to do what I thought they would do, what I knew they would do.'

'What? You knew they would have sex?'

'Yes, well, I knew they were having an affair, and I thought if I gave them the opportunity, they would incriminate themselves.'

I remove my hand from hers and shuffle up a little more in my sitting position. 'What do you mean *incriminate* themselves?'

'I know Craig, well, knew him, well enough to predict what he would do if the opportunity arose, and I was going to take advantage of it.'

'You knew they were having an affair, and you drugged us both? Why, for god's sake?'

'I needed irrefutable proof they were having an affair, damning evidence that they would happily carry on in the same building that we were upstairs in, sleeping.'

'What did you do, Melissa?'

She pauses before responding.

'When everyone was upstairs getting ready to go out that night, I went back downstairs, unscrewed the white wines, laced both bottles with the sleeping pills, recapped them, and put them back in the chiller cabinet. I figured if we were both upstairs, in a deep sleep, in Craig's selfish mind, he would think we had drunk too much and wouldn't disturb him, and he would convince Tanya to sleep with him in the downstairs bedroom; he's always liked being daring, it adds to the excitement he used to say, so I gambled that if it were to happen, it would be in the third bedroom downstairs.'

'Is that why you chose that cottage? Because it had a third bedroom downstairs?

'Yes.'

'Wow, you planned it all, and?'

'Then they were killed... and, well… if I hadn't drugged the wine, maybe they would still be alive today, and I'm struggling with that.'

'The police would not have blamed you for Hatzis turning up and killing them… or… no, wait, no, tell me you didn't… you didn't arrange for him to come and kill them, *did you*?'

'No, I wouldn't do that!' she snaps at me curtly. 'Anyway, he didn't kill them.'

'What? Of course, he did.'

'He did? Did he?' she asks menacingly, 'Are you sure of that?'

'It's beyond doubt. He was there, in the bedroom. He even had a photograph on his phone that proved he was there. He fled the scene.'

She sits up slightly now, the fire softly illuminating her, and she looks at me. 'I didn't expect Hatzis to turn up, but he did, and it all worked out for the best in the end.'

'How can you possibly think Hatzis turning up worked out for the best in the end?'

'Well, I clearly had too much of the wine with crushed sleeping pills and was completely out of it. I didn't come around until later the following day in hospital. Then, when the police told me they had been murdered and first questioned me, I just said I couldn't remember anything; I said I was that drunk someone must have put me in my bed. I needed time to work out what to do and wait to see who knew what. They told me you were the prime suspect, and I knew it had to have been different; the amount of crushed sleeping pills we consumed meant we were out for the count, and there was no way either of us could have been involved.'

'I still don't get it; why did Hatzis turning up work out for the best in the end?'

'As I said, I needed proof of their affair, so…' pausing, squirming slightly and lowering her look from me, 'I put a wireless nanny cam in the bedroom to catch them on a video recording having sex.'

I jump at this information, and she draws back from me. I twist and look at her, 'You did WHAT?'

She sits upright in bed now and looks at me, 'I needed proof of their affair so that I could get a decent settlement in the divorce that would follow; Craig wouldn't want his precious reputation pasted across the internet, especially after recently making Partner.'

I'm freaked out by this; she had a nanny cam video the whole time and kept it secret. 'I can't believe you did that,' and I'm dreading asking for more information, but she did keep this secret from everyone, 'So where is the video then? Why didn't you give it to the police?' Why keep the video recording a secret?'

'Because, somehow, and I don't know how… *you* killed them.'

Her words hit me like a bucket of ice-cold water. 'What do you mean I killed them?'

'You were on the video; you entered the room, raised the sword high and plunged it into Craig's back, straight through him and into Tanya beneath him.'

'Me? No. That's not right, you're lying. I couldn't have done that; I'm not a killer.'

'Yes, but you did, it's true.'

'How can it possibly be true?'

'I know you did it; it was on the video, the recording was very clear, and you are easily recognisable.'

'Wait. So, if you have a video showing I did it, you've known this all along then?'

'More or less. Well, no, to be fair, it was a few days later after I was discharged from the hospital, before I could get to see the video, and that's when I realised it was you and that the police had the correct prime suspect. Look, when the police left after speaking with me in the hospital, I panicked; I had drugged us both, and this allowed some stranger to come into the cottage and kill them. But you were their prime suspect, and I knew that couldn't be right, but I couldn't own up to the nanny cam without incriminating myself with drugging the wine, and if I did that, the police might have thought I was involved with the killer, you know, pre-arranging it with them.'

'My god, Melissa. If you knew I'd killed them, then why didn't you just tell the police?'

'By the time I had viewed the video, Hatzis was already in the frame, and it was too good to be true. His turning up within half an hour of your killing them was a sign, so I took it; he had been at the cottage, in the bedroom; I had him on the video, a man with a previous record for violence, possibly linked to the gang that had threatened Craig, and he wasn't saying anything to the police; his dumb pride and loyalty to the gang getting in the way of him proving himself innocent. The police were convinced they had their man, so why change it?'

'But you could have proved he didn't do it and that I did. So, where is this video now?'

'I deleted the video and removed it from the cloud file, but the camera is still in the cottage, in the air vent in the end wall overlooking the bed.'

I'm struggling to take this in. Melissa has known all these months that I killed them, and yet, she has not let on to a soul. Or is this a line? Is she trying to convince me that I killed them? She says there's no video any longer, so how can she prove it was me? I have to ask her, 'Why? Why would you delete the video? Why not hand it over to the police? You knew the truth.'

'Because you were sleepwalking, and it was me drugging the wine that caused it. You just walked into the room and plunged the sword through them both; you were in automatic mode, showing no emotion; it was like you were in a trance or something. I think you simply stumbled upon them and just did what you did under instinct whilst sleepwalking, not even aware of what you had done. I checked out the possible side effects of the pills I used; they include, in rare cases, people doing things like sleepwalking or sleep driving to the extent that they cannot remember what they had done the next morning, and this can be exacerbated when mixed with alcohol; so, I caused it to happen. Hatzis turning up allowed me to use him to protect you.'

Looking into her eyes, I can see she is unsure whether she should have told me this or not; her eyes are pleading with me, or is it the realisation that she has just told a killer that she knows he is a killer and we're in a remote place with no one else around for miles? I need to calm her, reassure her what she did was the right thing and that I'm not that person she needs to worry about.

Taking hold of her hands, keeping my focus on her, 'I'm glad I stayed quiet now about what I knew. In my heart, I was convinced you couldn't have planned this with Hatzis. I just wouldn't believe you could take on a hired killer, but I did know it was you who drugged the wine. My head was putting two and two together and thinking that maybe you hired Hatzis, but I just couldn't figure out why.'

'You see, if you could have thought that, then so could the police.' She pauses, takes hold of my hand, and squeezes gently. 'How could you possibly know it was me?'

'Well, I know that I didn't drug the wine, so it had to be you.'

'Really, why me? Why not Tanya or Craig so that they could spend time together? That's what the police thought.'

'Because I have a medical condition, a reaction to certain medication, especially sleeping drugs. Tanya knew this from the treatment I was having over the last year. If Craig had drugged the wine without Tanya's knowledge, he would have told her to convince her that I was knocked out, or she wouldn't have gone ahead with it, at the risk of them being caught, and then, on hearing this, she would panic because of the reaction I could have had; Tanya obviously knew not to use sleeping pills.'

A look of concern flashed across her face as she quietly asked, 'So, if you knew I'd drugged the wine, why didn't *you* say something to the police?'

'Simply because I didn't know about the drugs at first. It was only after the police sampled the wine bottles and found residue in just the white wine bottles, and then identified the classification of drug that I knew it had to be you. Only the four of us knew that the two of us only drank white wine, and the other two would know about my drug reaction, leaving you as the only possible person. When I'd heard you were diagnosed with alcohol poisoning, at first, I thought there may have been more to it, as you, and I, for that matter, have a pretty high alcohol intake threshold, much higher than the drink we consumed that day and night. And then, like you, Hatzis fell into the frame supporting the threat made against Craig's life.'

'Well, if you knew I'd drugged the wine and a professional thug was involved, why didn't *you* tell the police of *your* suspicions that I could have arranged it all.'

'Why would I tell them? Craig turned out to be a right bastard; I never thought he would do that to me, sleep with my wife, with your friend, cheating on you, on us both; that is lower than low. Besides, up to you telling me that I killed them, I too thought Hatzis had done it, possibly with your involvement or not; Tanya and Craig got what they deserved, so why would I correct them?'

Remaining upright on the bed, highlighted by the flames of the fire, I could tell I had surprised her with my deduction that she spiked the wine. She knew I'd killed them, but she decided not to say anything to protect me and to protect herself, so now we have something on each other, and to be sure we both remain free, I need to expand on this for our collective benefit, and of course, my own self-protection, for mine is probably the greater crime; any prosecutor worth their salt would look to pin it on me as revenge for them having an affair.

I continue, 'Well, now we both know the truth and that we have both perverted the course of justice, we are both guilty of withholding vital information which, in your case, also directly led to the death of Hatzis in prison, the man you knew was innocent of the murders.'

'But… I thought…' she stutters.

'Thought what? You knew I was innocent of a wilful crime. I was operating on autopilot whilst sleepwalking, and for all we know, if you hadn't drugged me, then maybe things would have been different when Hatzis turned up. I might get some sympathy at trial as you did drug me, causing me to do what I did. If this comes out, we are both in a bad place; prosecuting counsel will have us down for life sentences now that you've destroyed the evidence that could have helped us both. We're in this together now.'

'Oh my god, I never really thought that I was the reason you killed them.' She drops her head in her hands, and I can see she is rocking slightly on the bed. She stops and looks up at me. 'And Hatzis died as well because I didn't say anything, I can't believe it. I must tell the police.'

'No, don't do that. Look, I'm not bothered about Hatzis; it sounds like he was scum anyway; he probably would have killed someone sooner or later; look on the bright side, you saved someone else. So, good riddance, he can take the fall for us, but we must stick together.' Looking at her and holding her hands tighter, I continue, 'I'm struggling with the fact that I killed them, though; I don't know how I could have done it. I can't remember any of it; I wouldn't hurt a fly. What did you drug us with?'

Melissa is whimpering quietly, mumbling something into her hands that I can't quite make out. 'What is it, Melissa? What are you saying?'

'I think we should go to the police,' she quietly replies, almost sheepishly, sounding like she wants me to talk her out of it.

'I know it's the right thing to do, just as you do, but it's the last thing we should do.' She's losing it, and I need to bring her back to her senses. 'Melissa, listen. Look at me. We can't change the past, but we can plan our future together. We must be careful, or we'll have no future.'

'Together?'

'Yes. What is done is done; we can't turn the clock back. The matter is closed for everyone else; we're the only two who knew what happened, and if we can learn to live with that, we can be happy, can't we?' I pause slightly, 'What do you think?'

'Could we? Could we really be happy together?'

'Why not? Come here,' releasing her hands, raising my outstretched arms to embrace her. She moves forward into my arms, and I hold her tight. 'We can be happy; I know we can. And we deserve to be.'

As I hold her, I wonder if I can trust her; she knows I did this, although innocently, and she would incriminate herself now if she told anyone what she knew had happened, and worse, she has destroyed the evidence. *Or has she?* Does she still have a copy of that video somewhere to hold over me at some future date? If she has it, is it secure? Can I trust her? I have no choice; for the time being, we must trust each other; we're in a surreal place now; it's mad, mutually assured destruction.

'Is the nanny cam still there, in the cottage?' I whisper to her.

'Yes,' her soft reply.

'Does it have a memory card in it, or is it just a wireless signal?'

'I'm not sure, why?'

'For us to be together, we need to recover the camera; it could still hold a video file of me sleepwalking.'

She sniffs lightly, 'Oh, yes, right, good point. I have the receipt for the camera somewhere in an email after I purchased it online; it'll indicate the type or model number. We could check it now if you want.'

'Yes, we should check it out as that'll be the only thing that could ruin our future together, as it will show Hatzis didn't do it. However, we'll have to drive off to pick up a decent signal to check your emails; we'll go after breakfast tomorrow, and if it has a memory card, we'll have to work out how to get the camera back.'

'Yes, OK. I'm sorry, Martin, I caused all of this.'

She's still with me then, that's good. 'No, don't be sorry. It's just something that happened that wasn't planned to end that way; we'll sort it out tomorrow, and then we can put it behind us.'

42

Melissa – the Bothy bedroom

Buried in his arms, snuggling tight into his chest, it feels safe, but he… no; it is safe; it has to be now. I knew who the real killer was and didn't tell the police and have since destroyed the video file. I let the police believe Hatzis was the killer, and they followed their own agenda there; that part is on them. Martin was surprised when I told him he had killed them and, at first, he didn't believe me, but then quickly seemed to accept that I was telling him the truth even though now I have no proof to show him or help his defence if he needs to; I suppose he fully trusts me. He knows I drugged the wine, and he could, through logic, convince the police that it was me that did it, and, if he did that, and the police still thought Hatzis was the killer, then in their eyes I would be the accomplice to Hatzis, not Martin. But now I know about his medical condition, which will explain his actions if I go to the police, but we could both suffer if I did that. I have to trust him, just like he has to, and is, trusting me.

His breathing is slow but deep, comforting. Good relationships are founded on trust; I remember reading that somewhere in a magazine or something. Do I think they mean founded on this kind of trust? Probably not, but if this is what we have left and want to be together, then why not? We can build on this foundation.

I pull away from his embrace and slide fully back beneath the duvet, lying on my side and turning towards him. He watches me as I snuggle down and raise my left arm for him to join me. He looks down at me, not moving like he's weighing up some major decision. In the firelight, I see him smile and nod slightly to himself as he slides down on the bed, remaining on top of the duvet, turning onto his side to embrace me. We lie still, listening to the wind and the crackling fire, just savouring the moment together.

Closing my eyes, my thoughts drift and play with our future; can we make it work? Together? What about his mood swings and his anger issues? Are these alcohol-driven events, or is he hiding some other deeper frustration? I know he suffered a period of deep depression last year that was due to the bad reviews on his last published book, but does he have some other fragile mental health issues I need to appreciate? Then again, who wouldn't have issues after all we have been through?

His breathing is slowing and deepening; it's so peaceful. I'm surprised he can sleep after learning he killed them and that I had a camera hidden away. We can do this together; we can build a future. Tomorrow will be the first day of the rest of our lives together; we should talk, plan, and set some goals and dreams. Where will we live? Shall we marry? Will he want children with me? Whoa, I need to slow down; I need to give him some time and space. Taking a slow, deep breath, I settle deeper into his strong arms, listening to his heartbeat and slow, comforting methodical rhythm. I could stay like this forever.

43

Detective Constable Joanna Hansen – the Bothy

Saturday, 27th April

Banging on the front door, there is no response, although both Martin's and Melissa's cars are here parked at the side. One of the uniformed constables, PC MacPherson, comes from around the back, and he indicates there is no other external door, and he can't see in through the windows. 'I suppose they could be out for a long walk somewhere,' he adds in a mellow Scottish accent.

'Possibly.' I try the door handle, depressing the latch with my thumb, and it releases the door from the frame. It's unlocked and opens slightly. 'OK, we're going in.' But as I go to take a step, I catch myself, 'It'll have to be you two first; I have no jurisdiction up here.'

'Er, yes, er, Ma'am,' MacPherson replies.

'Jo will do fine.' Looking at them both, 'Ready?'

'Yes, Jo,' in unison.

I open the door fully, and MacPherson announces our presence as police officers and that we are coming in. He enters first, followed by his female colleague, PC Hamer; I remain by the front door until they are both inside. I step in just over the threshold and notice the room is dim, a little warmer than outside, but the air feels heavy and stale. They're checking out the living room area and kitchen, and I offer guidance from the doorway, 'Pull back some curtains, will you, let the light in. I'll open the shutters outside'.

'Yes, Jo,' comes back the acknowledgement.

I go to the first shutter, which is the front window, and open the weathered wooden shutters, locking them back into the open position. As I head to the side window, MacPherson shouts something that I can't quite hear, so I return to the front door.

I see him slowly opening the bedroom door and take a tentative step forward into the room, announcing his presence. I walk in now, heading across the living room towards the bedroom, and on getting there, notice how much darker it is. The wooden window shutters are still closed, and my eyes are slowly transitioning from the bright sunlight outside to the low light of the interior. MacPherson reaches behind his back, removes a small torch from his utility belt, and clicks it on, instantly shouting out, 'In here!'

They are here, both lying on the bed, not moving, even with our presence entering the room, both having that deathly look on them that I've seen before. We rush over to the bed and eagerly check both for a pulse, looking for a glimmer of life to work with. But there is nothing, no breath, no pulse, no life; both are dead and look like they have been for some time.

'Bloody hell. Get some light in here, will you?'

Hamer runs back outside, and she opens the shutters to the bedroom window as MacPherson pulls back the curtains and he turns and asks, 'Shall I get an ambulance up here?'

'Yes, I suppose so, but it won't do much good. I'd better phone this in.'

I turn to leave the room, pulling out my mobile and scrolling the contacts list as I head for the front door. Hamer re-enters the living room as I leave the bedroom. We walk past each other, and I turn back to her, 'Seal the area; this could be a crime scene.'

'Yes, Jo.'

I find the number I'm after and tap the button, only to then realise I have no network connection. Just as I step out of the front door, PC Hamer calls out, 'I have a pulse! It's faint, but I have one!'

I turn and run back in towards the bedroom, 'My god, are you sure?'

'Yes.'

'Who?'

As I re-enter the bedroom, Hamer is standing beside him, loosening his clothing and trying to turn him into the recovery position but struggling due to his size, the soft bed and Martin embracing her, Melissa. 'Nicholson,' she replies.

I look at MacPherson, 'Do you have a helicopter up here? A flying doctor or paramedics or something?'

'Mountain Rescue Team uses the RAF Search & Rescue helicopter from the base up the coast. They can get a medic here quicker than the nearest hospital. I'll call them now!' he shouts out as he runs out of the bedroom.

Hamer shouts after him, 'Get me the bag!'

Standing beside Hamer, we struggle to roll Martin together. That's when I register that he is lying on top of the duvet, and Melissa is underneath it; I must note these facts as we're destroying the scene trying to save him. We get him into the recovery position as MacPherson returns.

'They're on their way. I need to find a clearing for the helicopter to land. Here, take this,' and he hands a large green kit bag to me, and I pass it to Hamer.

She wastes no time in unzipping the large bag on the floor, pulling the two halves open. Inside, there is a small oxygen bottle and mask, along with all kinds of other medical aid materials. She passes the bottle and mask to me, saying, 'Get this on him quickly; it'll help.'

I pull the elastic strap over his head and place the mask over his mouth and nose. Turning the small valve on the top of the bottle, the release of oxygen is instantaneous. I look across at her, and she is checking his pulse again.

After a minute or so, she says, 'It's improving; definitely a pulse there now,' nodding to herself.

'Excellent, great work, Hamer, well done.'

'We get lots of this up here, although usually when old folk mix with those things over there, they're a bad combination,' she replies as she flips her thumb over her shoulder. I look past her and see the log burner.

'What, the fire?'

'Yep. I'll put fifty pounds on it being carbon monoxide poisoning. Can you see if the window will open?'

'Sure.' As I turn, her manner is surprising. She takes charge quickly with instructions while I'm opening the window, and she continues.

'Sorry, we need to act fast in such cases. I'd better check her again.' I watch Hamer move around the bed and carefully recheck Melissa, placing her fingers on three different pulse points on Melissa. After about a minute or so, she turns to me, frowning, slightly shaking her head from side to side, 'No.'

'You've come across this before?'

Hamer returns to Martin and rechecks his pulse. 'Yes, unfortunately, it's why we started carrying these kit bags. Holiday homes, old buildings, campfires inside derelict buildings, we get a few incidents up here each year.'

'You're well trained.'

'Yes, I spent five years in the Ambulance service before I decided to switch to the police. I wanted a change, go figure.'

'It's a good job it was you; MacPherson and I missed it.'

'It takes practice and experience; such a shallow pulse can easily be missed.'

MacPherson comes back into the room. 'The helicopter is at least fifteen minutes away. Can he hang on until then?'

Hamer replies, 'Yes, he's in good hands,' as she opens a small packet and starts to unfold a foil thermal blanket to cover him with.

44

Martin – Borders Royal Hospital

Late afternoon, Saturday 27th April

It seems it is my turn to wake up in a hospital bed now, but I'm not sure what I'm doing here. I have an oxygen monitor attached to the middle finger of my left hand and a nasal oxygen tube to my nostrils with the feed pipes running behind my ears; they're irritating me, and I want to remove them.

As I move to sit up, a nurse enters the room and, in a soft Scottish accent, speaks to me, 'Good afternoon, Martin. How are you feeling?'

Before I can respond, she is at my side, helping me sit up and rearranging the pillows behind my back.

'Where am I? Why am I here?'

'You are in the Borders Royal Hospital in Melrose, Scotland. You inhaled an almost fatal quantity of carbon monoxide; any longer, and you probably would not have survived. It was lucky the police officers that found you had some good medical training; they got to you just in time.'

'What do you mean police officers that found me? What is going on?'

She stops moving the pillows and steps back to look at me. As she does so, two people enter the room. It is like one of those scenes you hear about when everything rushes back to you, and I recall the discussions with Melissa, and now the police are here. What has she gone and done? Has she drugged me again? The two of us could have worked this out together.

'Is it OK if I talk to Mr Nicholson now?' one of the strangers asks, again in a Scottish accent but much deeper and a little harsher.

I figure the question is directed at the nurse rather than me.

'Yes, he should be OK, but nothing too strenuous. Mr Nicholson is recovering well, but take it easy,' replies the nurse.

'Thank you,' from this stranger. They both approach my bedside and look at me, 'Hello, Mr Nicholson. I'm Detective Sergeant Watts, and this is my colleague from England, Detective Constable Hansen, with the West Ryshire Constabulary. How are you feeling, Sir?'

'I'm not sure to be honest. What is going on? Why are you here?'

Watts replies, 'This incident happened under Scottish jurisdiction, and given the circumstances, and the background information provided by DC Hansen, the Crown Office and Procurator Fiscal Service has requested a formal investigation into this incident. It was my colleague here, DC Hansen, who found you yesterday, and she is assisting us with our fatal accident inquiry.'

'Fatal? What are you talking about?'

I see the female DC look at the DS, and he nods slightly. Then, she turns to me. 'I came to visit you at your cabin with a couple of colleagues yesterday, and we found you unconscious inside the building, apparently a victim of carbon monoxide poisoning. What can you remember? Can you recall anything?'

'My cabin, you mean my Bothy. Er, well, yes, I can, some of it anyway. I was with my friend Melissa. I remember we were talking and… I don't know, maybe I fell asleep.'

'Were you talking in the bedroom?

'Yes, I think so. Yes, we were lying on the bed just talking and… hang on, where is she? Is she OK? Is she in here also?' As I ask the questions, the English Detective looks uncomfortable, clearing her throat, but the Detective Sergeant replies.

'No. Martin, I'm sorry to inform you that your friend Melissa Tyler didn't make it. She was found dead beside you.'

'What? No, that can't be. We were just chatting and…'

So, Melissa didn't call the police then, and now she's dead; well, that solves one of my problems; I won't have to worry about what Melissa saw now. Wow, I can't believe I just thought that knowing that she was the one who protected me, and we were planning a future together, what is wrong with me?

He continues, 'Yes, I'm afraid so. We have been in touch with her family, and they are on their way up here as we speak.'

The English Detective then speaks, 'Can I ask why you were both at your Bothy?'

'Sorry, I'm confused; why did you come up from West Ryshire to my Bothy? It's in the middle of nowhere.'

'I'll come to that in a moment; I just need to know why you were both there… Martin?'

'I was writing, taking a few days away from the distractions of home and town life; I was working on my latest novel.'

'So, you were working, making the most of the peace and quiet,' she continues.

'Yes. I used to spend quite a bit of time writing in my Bothy, and after all the things that have happened, I needed somewhere to go; I needed to see if I could get back into writing.'

'So, if you were there for the solitude if you don't mind my asking, then why was Melissa with you?'

'Actually, I think I do mind. You've just told me we were gassed and that my friend is dead from the same stuff that nearly killed me, and now you're asking me questions about why she was there. I'm getting a bad feeling of déjà vu here; am I under suspicion for something again, something I didn't do? It's not that long ago, I became the prime suspect in the double murder of my wife and friend, and that turned out to be nothing to do with me. Is that how you people work: find the nearest person to the scene and then accuse them? For god's sake!' I could feel a rage building in me, my volume rising, and I could see her feeling it.

The DS looks at the DC quizzically, no doubt wondering what I am ranting on about, but the nurse quickly intervenes, 'That's enough. Mr Nicholson, it would be best if you remained calm; you're still suffering the effects of the carbon monoxide. Now, Detectives, I think it's time for you to leave, don't you?'

The Detective Constable looks at the nurse with raised eyebrows, but the DS intervenes, 'Yes, I suppose it is. Mr Nicholson, we will need to talk again; we'll return tomorrow.'

'Do I need my solicitor present again?'

But before he replies, the English Detective interjects, clearly overstepping the mark with the DS: 'No, you are not a suspect or anything like that. We just need to find out what happened at your Bothy. But, of course, if you want your solicitor present, then that is your prerogative.'

The DS speaks, directing his words to his English companion, 'Come on, we're leaving. Now.'

They leave the room with her comment hanging in the air. Does she know something? Did Melissa say something to the police before she died? Does this Detective suspect something isn't quite right?

'Don't mind her; they're all the same, these detectives,' the nurse says softly beside me. 'Now, let's get you laid down again; get you some more rest.'

45

DC Jo Hansen – Borders Royal Hospital

Sunday, 28th April

Walking the hospital corridor back to the private room shadowing my Scottish chaperone, DS Watts, the thoughts return to me again, wrestling and not resting. What is it to be? I can't make up my mind. Either Martin is a very lucky individual, or he's very unlucky; I can't decide which. I still can't decide whether he's involved in the deaths that surround him or if he's a victim of what has happened to those near him. His wife and best friend were having an affair and were murdered by a stranger whilst they were having sex downstairs when he was upstairs unconscious, unwittingly drugged with sleeping meds. He's now survived another close call with death when his friend, Melissa, died beside him; it being her husband who drugged them that night before he was murdered. Is it me, or do some people live in a perpetual state of chaos?

We had the man for the double murders, and I don't think anyone is stupid enough to use carbon monoxide as a screen to pretend to nearly die; it is so unpredictable, as shown by Melissa's death. I suppose then he's simply a mix of both lucky and unlucky; I guess some people are like that.

My seniors want to close the file on this now; there are plenty of other crimes to address. However, I think I'll give it just one last crack and see if I can unnerve him enough to slip up or expose a weakness; it's just that it bugs me, and I don't know why.

Detective Sergeant Watts has agreed to let me have some latitude with questions, as clearly, I know more of the previous events in England and was present in the Bothy when we found them as we did, but he was clear that the primary action is to obtain his formal statement for their investigation into Melissa's now suspicious death.

As we approach the private room, the door is open, and stepping into the room, Martin is standing by his bed, dressed, and packing a small bag.

I don't wait to introduce ourselves, 'Good morning, Martin; are you being discharged already?'

He looks up at us, 'Morning, Detective Hansen, Detective Sergeant Watts; yes, the doctors are happy for me to leave. I am to take it easy for the next few days, though, and I'll make a full recovery.'

The DS speaks, clearly frustrated with me cutting across him once again, 'Good morning, Mr Nicholson; I need to take your formal statement before you return home; shall we do it here or at the Station?'

'If we must, then we can do it here. Please don't take offence at this, Sergeant, but I don't relish the idea of returning to a police station anytime soon. I'm sure your colleague here has since brought you up to speed with past events.'

'Yes, she has, and no, I suppose I see your point. Shall we?' indicating the chairs beside the bed.

I turn and pull one of the plastic chairs to me, and I sit. It feels like I'm becoming the outsider now; suddenly, these two are developing a little rapport.

The DS starts, 'Now, moving on from our discussion yesterday, have you remembered anything that could add to what happened?'

'No, I haven't. It's like I said, I was already at my Bothy working, and Melissa arrived unannounced out of the blue. She wanted to see how I was doing and wanted to see if we were still talking to each other.'

'Why would she think you weren't?' I ask, noticing the DS shake his head slightly as he writes on his pad.

'After everything that happened, I pulled back, retreated into myself, and kind of cut myself off from everyone; I just wanted some time and space to process.'

'But she stayed with you at the Bothy; you were happy with that, I mean, her arriving "*out of the blue*" and interrupting your time?' I continue.

'Yes, actually, I was. I was pleasantly surprised to see her.'

'And what did you talk about?'

'I can't see how what we talked about is any of your concern, Detective, save to say we talked as old friends, we cried, we laughed together.'

OK, I'll push some now, let's see what happens, 'Were you two a couple? Were you sleeping together?'

'Sorry? How dare you! No, we weren't.'

The DS interrupts, 'Apologies for my English colleague, Mr Nicholson; she does have her own investigation in hand, which is overlapping my investigation. I'm sure the Detective Constable will respect that.'

That was clearly me being put in my place by Watts, but I continue with my original strategy. 'Well, it's just that when we found you, the two of you were in bed together.'

'No, no, we weren't in bed together, Detective Constable. Melissa was under the duvet, and I was on top of it; yes, I'm sure I was. We'd had a disagreement, and I went to the bedroom to apologise to her. I was on top of the bed covers. We weren't a "thing", and your suggestion that we were is offensive.'

I knew this; I recall him holding her from on top of the covers, both fully dressed. I just wanted to gauge his reaction. 'I'm sorry, I didn't mean to suggest…'

'But you did, didn't you!' he snaps back at me.

'OK, let's just take a second or two, shall we?' the DS says.

I don't speak for a minute or so, feigning I'm writing down something important in my notebook. Without looking up from my notes, 'You seem to have a short fuse, Martin. Is that what caused the two of you to have a disagreement? What did you argue about?'

He sighs deeply before answering, 'We didn't argue as such; it was about nothing really; we would both touch a nerve or something, and it would flare up. The nurse mentioned this morning that one of the effects of carbon monoxide poisoning on a person is to induce irritability, develop mood swings, invoke a short temper. Maybe that's what was behind us having words, I don't know. Now, if we're done, Detectives, I want to get out of here.' He stands from the chair.

The DS cuts in, 'Mr Nicholson, I'm sorry, but I do need a formal statement from you. Maybe it'll be better if you did call into the Police Station later today so we can conclude that. I'm sure the Detective Constable here will need to return south for other pressing matters.'

I know when I'm being closed down, so I have one last opportunity now.

'Just a couple more things, some of which I think will be of interest to you, Martin.' Standing looking at me, he sighs and sits back down again. The DS sighs also.

'What? What more is there to this?' Martin asks.

'I've been going over the case files related to the murders back in June last year, and something new has come to light.'

'What could possibly be new?'

'Well, when you were assisting us with our enquiries...'

'Oh, that's what you call it, is it, *assisting you*?'

I ignore his comment and continue, 'If you recall, we took some blood samples from you, and we also took some from Melissa; I presume the SIO was interested in the amount of alcohol you had both consumed.'

'And?'

'Well, yes, you both had elevated alcohol levels, but you also had elevated levels of the same sleeping substance in your samples.'

'And?'

The DS is sitting back with his arms folded, listening and observing.

'It seems someone wanted the two of you quietly out of the way, and well, who would? And how could they get it into your system without the two of you realising it? I looked over the scene photographs and noted the bottles of wine, so I recalled all the bottles from the evidence store and had them tested; the white wine bottles both showed up positive for trace samples of a prescribed sedative, but only the white wine bottles. The only people drinking white wine were you and Melissa; hence, as Craig and Tanya were having an affair, I suggest that they drugged the bottles of white wine, an easy step to make sure they wouldn't be affected.'

'Yes, and? This isn't new.'

'No, but it formed part of the reason you were charged with attempted murder.'

'Which was nonsense, and you know that. Craig or Tanya, or both, did it so they could get us out of the way.'

'Yes, but I just find that a little convenient. The person or persons responsible for that are dead and can't attest to whether or not they did it.'

'I'm not sure I'm following you here, Detective.'

'With you upstairs fast asleep for hours, it gave them the opportunity to be together downstairs. Apparently, their affair had been going on for some time.' I pause, letting this information sink in. He is sitting quietly, and I can almost hear his mind ticking away. 'Does that surprise you, Martin, that it wasn't spontaneous, that it was planned?'

'Nothing surprises me anymore. As it turned out, they were partly to blame for their own deaths,' looking at me with a blank expression on his face.

'No, you can't put their deaths on them; that was Hatzis. Looking at this logically, the only two cars outside the cottage were Craig's Range Rover and Tanya's Volvo. Somehow, Hatzis knew they were at the cottage for a weekend away; I don't know how, a tip-off, someone knew, whatever, and only seeing their two cars outside, he came in and killed them, then left. You and Melissa were lucky, really; if he knew you were upstairs, he would probably have killed the two of you as well.'

'I can't believe they drugged Melissa and me just so they could have sex that night like they couldn't wait for another time. It does seem irrational. Oh, wait; do you think it was Melissa that tipped Hatzis off?'

'No. Why would you think she'd do that?'

I could sense him joining jigsaw pieces up and forming pictures in his mind, and he continues, 'Well, it was Melissa that made the reservation. Wait… if Melissa knew they were having an affair, she could have drugged the white wine and set this whole thing up with Hatzis; she knew there was a spare bedroom downstairs, and Hatzis went straight to that room.'

I cast a glance at the DS, who is looking at Martin. The DS has a slightly astonished look on his face, which is natural, I suppose, as this does all sound a little convoluted to someone hearing it for the first time. I continue.

'Granted, but that seems a little farfetched, although it could have happened that way. The trouble is, now we'll never know; both Hatzis and Melissa are dead, and nothing points to them knowing each other or being in contact together; I've checked.'

'Umm, OK, I agree; I don't think Melissa would kill them or arrange for them to be killed; it wasn't in her nature. So, what is it you're saying, Detective, what's changed?'

He's moved quickly to the past tense with Melissa, or am I overthinking this? 'Nothing, I suppose; I just wasn't sure you knew they were in a long-term relationship with each other.'

He's not biting; maybe he didn't have anything to do at all with this. 'We still maintain Hatzis was working under orders from Costas or one of his lieutenants.'

'Oh, right, well, that makes sense.'

I jot a note down in my book again as he makes a good point about Melissa that I hadn't fully considered; I then flick a couple of pages backwards, and before I speak, he gets in before me.

'I don't think you said why you came up to my Bothy Detective? Why did you? Not for this, surely? And how did you know I was there?'

Well, I did want to push him a little to see if he would let anything slip; let's try another angle. 'I have been looking into things a little deeper, and I wanted to talk with you about something that concerned me, but I couldn't contact you, your mobile was just going to voice message. I spoke with your publishers, and they informed me you were working from your Bothy, and because I couldn't speak with you, I needed to make sure you were OK.'

'Really? Why?'

I'll need to roll this out slowly as there could be a simple and innocent explanation for all this, and I don't want to add to his anguish, 'You did most of the work on the Bothy refurbishment yourself, is that correct?'

Out of the corner of my eye, I note that the DS is sitting up a little in his chair as we return to the reason he's here.

'Er, yes,' Martin replies.

'And you have a carbon monoxide monitor in the Bothy, but it wasn't working; can you explain that to us?'

'No, it is relatively new. I only bought it early last year, I think. Is it faulty?'

The DS is writing on his pad now.

'Well, you could say that as the batteries had been removed.'

'Really? Well, I didn't remove them; it would be useless without them.'

'So, you didn't remove the batteries to use in a torch or something and simply forgot to replace them?'

'No, I didn't.'

'Umm, so, if you didn't remove them, who did?'

'What? You think Melissa took them out?'

'Well, one reason to remove them would be that the alarm wouldn't go off as a warning.'

'Do you think the carbon monoxide thing was Melissa, some kind of suicide pact? That she was struggling and decided she'd had enough and, knowing of my troubles, decided to take me with her?'

'Possibly, the thought had occurred to me. But for a plan like this to work as a lethal weapon, somebody would still have to tamper with the fire or chimney so that sufficient carbon monoxide gases would escape into the room rather than up through the chimney flue.'

I can hear the DS's pen racing across paper.

'Well, I don't think Melissa would have had the opportunity to be honest,' Martin replies.

'So, you didn't leave her alone at any point, step outside, go for a walk on your own?'

'Well, yes, I did, but she wasn't my prisoner and I trusted her. No, I don't think Melissa wanted either of us to die, never mind die together; we were talking of the future. Anyway, what has this got to do with you taking my statement and coming up to my Bothy? It sounds more like a formal police interview this.'

The DS looks up, and before he speaks, I ignore Martin's comment and continue, 'Umm, I tend to agree with you; I don't see Melissa wanted this outcome for the two of you. As I said, I have been digging a little deeper into this, doing a bit more detective work.'

'And?'

'Can you think of anyone that would want *you* dead? Someone that would benefit from you dying?'

'Me? No, not that I can think of.' He pauses for a second or two. 'I have no enemies; the only benefit of my dying would be life insurance, I suppose; is that what you're thinking of?'

'It could be, as you do have quite generous policy coverage on yourself, and on Tanya for that matter, I've checked.'

'Well, Tanya has been dead for months now, and I've still not replied to the insurance company's letters and emails; it's been the furthest thing from my mind.'

'Yes, I know; I spoke with your Insurers, and they said the same. But what I did discover was that Tanya had been in touch with them and then with the legal firm that looks after your wills; she wanted to know, if you passed, what would happen to your backlist of published works.'

'Well, it would all transfer to her.'

'Yes, that's what your solicitor said as well.'

'Hang on a minute; are you now insinuating that Tanya tinkered with the fires and removed the batteries from the monitor to what… bump me off? How on earth does she do that from the grave?'

The DS stops writing and looks up at Martin, then at me.

'Three weeks before you had that fateful trip to the holiday cottage, Tanya and Craig drove up here and spent a night in a small Inn about twenty miles away. They could easily have detoured here to fix the fires/chimneys and remove the batteries.'

'Really? What, and you can prove this?'

'Yes, you thought Tanya was away on a work conference; it's in your diary, and the owner of the Inn recognised their photos; he was convinced they were having an affair as they were "*too attentive*" in his words, "*married couples are not like that*", and the gentleman bought the most expensive bottle of red wine we had available, "*certainly not a couple easily forgotten,*" he said. So, I checked the GPS coordinates of your Bothy and found that they were on the recently visited list in Craig's satnav in his Range Rover.'

'The scheming basta…'

I cut in before he finishes, 'My colleagues here in Scotland have had the carbon monoxide monitor tested for prints and, whilst it wouldn't be a surprise to find Tanya's fingerprints on it, we did find a clear print from Tanya on the inside of the battery cover; she had clearly opened the monitor at some point, and I would expect if it was empty of batteries then, she would have questioned that with you. That said, she could have, of course, simply removed the batteries because she needed them for something at the time and forgot to replace them; again, it's impossible to confirm now.'

From a body language point of view, this certainly looks like news to him; his reaction and expressions are of surprise. If he didn't know they were having an affair and planning his demise, then he had no reason to kill them. He would not have gambled with his and Melissa's lives if he removed the batteries, and I don't think Melissa had it in her to take her own life and his. Anyway, that clear fingerprint on the inside lid speaks volumes to me and to my boss when I informed him, especially when coupled with Tanya's trip to the Bothy with Craig. I make a mental note to ask the DS, although I suspect he'll be on this now, to get some technical people to look at the vents, chimneys, and flues to see if they have been tampered with; he will need chapter and verse on the installations, to understand why they were faulty for his investigation.

Martin is motionless. He is sitting looking at me, almost staring, looking straight through me; it's as though I'm not here in front of him. It's dawning on him that his wife, with her lover, had set in motion a sequence of events to kill him that very nearly did kill him. Unfortunately, that same plan killed Melissa almost a year after they visited Martin's Bothy to set the scene. Tampering with the fires to expel carbon monoxide inside the Bothy was cleverly conceived, and if Martin had visited the Bothy on his own some time afterwards, he would probably have died, and his death certified as an unfortunate accident; the result of poor renovation work carried out by Martin himself.

He's clearly shocked. 'Martin, are you OK?'

46

Martin – Borders Royal Hospital

Tanya and Craig planned to kill me? Me? The bloody nerve of the two of them. Well then, they definitely got their just reward.

'Tanya hadn't been up to my Bothy in ages, not since I first bought it, certainly not since I bought that gas detector. You really think they planned to kill me?' I ask the Detective before looking at the DS.

She replies, 'It'll be hard to prove now, but I would say there is sufficient indication that it is not inconceivable. There is certainly some compelling evidence, even more so now that you mention she hasn't been to your Bothy since you started work on it, although being unable to question them is a problem. Did you know they were having an affair?'

'No. I loved her, and I thought she loved me.'

'I'm sorry to break this to you like this, especially after the news of Melissa, your friend, passing.'

'So, Craig and Tanya became murderers after they were murdered last year. Wow, this is surreal.'

The DS raises his eyebrows slightly, then jots further notes in his pad.

'It seems you've had a very lucky escape, Martin, twice,' the Detective replies.

'I know, it does, doesn't it? Poor Melissa, innocent in all of this.' I say it knowing full well Melissa drugged the wine; why let the police know this now? What could possibly be gained by it? It would plausibly have given Melissa a reason to attempt suicide and take me with her, I suppose. Still, the Detective is pretty sure that Tanya and Craig tampered with the carbon monoxide monitor and fires in a plan to kill me. God, I have been lucky.

'Yes. Quite.'

She closes her notebook and stands, 'I'm not sure how much we can prove, but the authorities up here will be looking into Melissa's death, and I expect they will want a further investigation into Tanya and Craig and their movements before they died, but I'm fairly confident Melissa's death will end up being either declared accidental or left as an open verdict as proving pre-meditation could be a problem, given their own untimely deaths. This will all fall to my Scottish colleagues here, and we'll be happy to assist them.' She looks at the DS, still sitting.

The DS looks up and realises the discussion is probably finished for now. He closes his pad and pockets his pen to the inside of his jacket before standing.

'Er, yes, we will. I'm sorry, Mr Nicholson, but I will need you to call into the station before you head home today; we will need that formal statement from you. You're not planning to leave the country any time soon, are you?'

'Scotland or the UK?'

He looks at me, 'The UK, Sir.'

'No, I have nothing planned just yet. I'll drop into the station this afternoon.' As they turn to head out of the room, I add, 'Melissa and her family deserve more than an open verdict; for sure, it wasn't accidental.'

The English Detective turns back to me, 'Yes, well, all those who played a part in this are now dead. You are the only survivor, Martin.'

'Why is it that when you say it like that, it feels like you think I had some kind of a role in all of this? I'm a victim here; you do see that, don't you?'

'I'm Sorry, yes, I do. It was a bad choice of words on my part. I apologise.'

I don't know if that was a sincere apology or not; it came across as a little too scripted and too cold.

I sigh deeply, 'No. It feels like you think I'm involved in this, like I orchestrated it all, but how could I? Craig is embroiled in some major construction insurance scam or fraud, and an organised crime group threatens Craig, then next they decide to kill him using Hatzis, but Hatzis gets a bit overzealous, killing both Tanya and Craig; Hatzis then commits "*suicide*" in prison during his trial, more like murdered to silence him if you ask me; and then Tanya and Craig from the grave, inadvertently kill Melissa whilst trying to kill me. And you think I'm lucky? I've lost everyone close to me, my wife and my two best friends; I've been a prime suspect for a double murder and an attempted murder, and now the one place that is dear to me, my Bothy, I'll never return to again as it will haunt me. That's a fairly weird interpretation of being lucky, Detective.'

'Look, I'm sorry. I think it's best I leave now; let you finish packing, provide your statement to the DS here and then go home,' she replies.

'Ha, home. For god's sake, are you so densely insensitive?'

The DS turns to me, 'Er, Sir, no need for that; we have a job to do. There is an unexplained death, and the Procurator Fiscal requires answers.'

Before I can reply, Detective Constable Hansen looks at me and says, 'Goodbye, Martin. No doubt we'll be in touch again,' and she turns away from me.

Without another word, they leave the room, closing the door behind them. Sitting back in the chair, I pull my hands to my face, covering my cheeks and eyes.

This isn't over yet, is it? She said the Scottish police will continue to investigate further and that she will assist them as may be required. Will this ever end?

Melissa's camera! What could that do if it's found in the cottage? Someone will find it one day. Melissa planted it for a valid reason, a reason I know of but have not disclosed to the police; I haven't even mentioned its existence. She was only trying to do the right thing to help her get a divorce from Craig, but it filmed the events of that night. She said she had wiped the video from it, but has she? We never did conclude whether the camera had a video card in it or not. Damn it! And I bet she has left her fingerprints all over it; that is something this Detective will test for if the police find out about its existence. I need to recover that camera for two obvious reasons: to make sure there is no video of me killing them and to stop the police thinking Melissa was in cahoots with Hatzis, which I know she wasn't. If the police find it, they could try to tie me in with Melissa, suggesting we were also in a relationship together, which we weren't, and that we had planned all this so we could be together. Finding us together in my Bothy will add circumstantial, if not persuasive, argument to that theory. This morning, I thought this was all settled, and I could get on with my life, but that camera could be the one thing that could bring this whole sorry mess crashing down around me.

I've got to get my hands on that camera, but how?

47

Martin – Home in Northampton

Thursday, 2nd May

It's been nearly eleven months since the night Tanya and Craig died, and the police seem to have stopped with questions and statements in my direction. This morning, the Sheriff published her Determination into Melissa's death following the postmortem examination, citing death by carbon monoxide poisoning, and the Procurator Fiscal with the Scottish Police, no doubt acting on the information provided by DC Hansen and her colleagues, are continuing with their formal investigation into Melissa's death.

The Crown Office and Procurator Fiscal Service informed Melissa's family of their actions as her death is likely not to have been the result of the simple but avoidable accident that it first appeared to be, indicating that others, presumably Craig and Tanya, may have tampered with the fires and carbon monoxide monitor with malice aforethought; malice originally intended for me. And so, it continues.

That hidden camera's existence keeps playing over and over in my head, and with the police looking elsewhere for the time being, this seems like a good opportunity to try to get my hands on it. The easiest way would be to book out the cottage again for a long weekend, but that would look odd if I did it, and I have no one else that I could ask to do this for me; besides, only I know of the camera, and it must stay like that; I must do this myself.

I have a simple plan to gain access to the cottage, and I just need to get it rolling with the cottage owner. I tap in the number for the holiday let company on my mobile and the owner picks up in a couple of rings.

'Good morning, Escape Cottages. How can I be of assistance?'

'Ah, yes, good morning. My name is Martin Nicholson. I stayed at Fell View Cottage last year with some friends, and I have a rather unusual request, if I may?'

'Yes, of course. What is it?'

'I presume you still own and rent out the Cottage?'

'Yes, we do. Are you interested in renting it?'

It's clear he has not twigged who I am and my involvement with the cottage back then. 'Yes, well, I don't want to rent it as such; I just want to visit it.'

'Oh, I see; are you one of those real crime enthusiasts or something? One of those armchair detectives?'

'No, no, not at all; you see, er, my doctor has suggested it may help with my recovery.'

'Your doctor; help with your recovery, how?'

The line is silent for a few seconds. 'Oh my god, Martin Nicholson, I'm so sorry,' he says with a dawning realisation. Forgive me. You are the gentleman who was staying there at the time of the murders. I'm so sorry. I just remember the surname Tyler that it was booked under. Oh my, please forgive me.'

'No, it's fine; honestly, there's nothing to forgive. You see, I've been having trouble sleeping and bouts of depression, and my psychiatrist has suggested if I return to the cottage, it may help me overcome some of the issues and thoughts I've been having. To be frank, I'm not so sure, but I thought I'd give it a go to see if it'll help me.'

'Oh, I see. Yes, well, if you think it will, then I'm happy to assist you. How long do you think you need in the cottage?'

'Not long, maybe just a couple of hours.'

'Ah, OK, in that case, could you come to the cottage on a changeover day? It's just that, well, it's fully booked out now for the next few months.'

'Yes, I can do that. I can make that work, although I'll need the cottage just to myself, with no interruptions. Is that possible?'

'Yes, I can arrange that. I'll speak with the housekeeping team, and I'll make sure they are there as soon as the weekend occupiers leave. They can be finished in a couple of hours; that should leave you maybe two to three hours before the next occupiers arrive. Will that work for you?'

'It will, thank you. That's very accommodating of you.'

'Anything to help. Are you able to be at the cottage this next Monday, at, say, midday?'

'Yes, I can be, thank you. Will housekeeping let me in?'

'No, don't worry about access. I'll be in the area next Monday. I'll let you in, and then I'll return to lock up after you leave.'

'Thank you. Sorry, I didn't catch your name?'

'Rory, Rory Fraser.'

'Thank you, Rory. I'll see you there at midday next Monday.'

'Yes. Have a good weekend, Sir,' he replies, and I end the call.

Now that I have that sorted, I may as well get in touch with the insurance company and see what I need to do regarding Tanya's life insurance settlement; nodding to myself, the time has come for me to take control of my life and plan my future.

They were interesting comments he had just made; the cottage has been fully booked out since the murders and asking if I was one of those real crime enthusiasts. It takes all sorts; whatever floats your boat, I suppose.

48

Martin – Return to Fell View Cottage

Monday Morning, 6th May

As I turn into the short gravel driveway of the cottage, flashes of recall come to me. The cottage doesn't look any different, and why should it? I am a little concerned that this return to the place could actually have a negative effect on me, but I need to do it; I need that camera.

Approaching a parked Land Rover, I see who I presume to be, Rory sitting in the driver's seat. He looks up from his phone and raises his hand in a slight wave before opening the driver's door to step out.

I park alongside him and walk around my car to meet him.

'Good morning, Rory, is it?'

'Yes. I'm pleased to meet you, Mr Nicholson,' he says, pushing out his right hand to greet me.

'It's Martin,' and we shake hands. 'Thank you for this. I must admit, I never thought I'd be back here.'

'No, I suppose not.'

'So, the next occupiers are due at three o'clock today?'

'Yes, well, actually, I called them yesterday and suggested they make it more like four o'clock; I said we had a plumber doing a little maintenance, and they were fine with that.'

'Well, thank you, although I should be done in a couple of hours; I just want to walk through the rooms, maybe sit down and think things over a little, you know.'

'I understand; it's not a problem. I apologise again for not recalling your name last week and suggesting you may have been one of those real crime enthusiasts.' He turns towards the cottage, stepping toward the front door, continuing to speak, 'As you can imagine, after the mur..., er, incident, we have had some weird visitors. There were naturally quite a lot of cancellations following the incident, but now we seem to attract some of the more macabre visitors who want to spend time in a house where people were killed. Apparently, the cottage is on some kind of darker web page of places to stay overnight; go figure, eh?'

He inserts the key, unlocks the door, pushes it open, and turns to face me. I'm standing looking at him, and it dawns on him that he's been chunnering on about stuff that I probably don't want to hear; it's like he's excited about meeting a celebrity or something.

Looking squarely at him, I reply, 'Well, it takes all sorts, I suppose,' and I see his expression change instantly.

'Oh look, I'm sorry, me and my mouth,' apologising again, lowering both arms to his side in a kind of submissive gesture. 'Please,' he continues as he takes a step aside and indicates that I should enter the cottage. 'If you call my mobile about fifteen minutes before you're ready to leave, I'll pop back and lock up after you.'

Walking forward to enter the cottage, I pass across the front of him and reply, 'Yes, I will do; thank you, Rory.'

I step inside and feel an instant chill, unsure whether it's due to an actual temperature change or it's psychological from the events that occurred here, and I'm about to relive them. Behind me, I hear the Land

Rover door close and the engine start, and as I walk deeper into the cottage, the crushing sound of tyres on gravel fades as Rory pulls away. Then silence. The cottage interior is dimly lit, and I flick on the overhead lights, bringing life to the main living room and kitchen area. There is a light aroma of cleaning agent lingering, and I see the welcome bottle of wine and fresh bread on the breakfast bar, the same we found when we first arrived here nearly a year ago. I return to the front door, close it and feel the chill fading. Weirdly, I'm starting to feel excited, possibly heightened adrenalin, in the knowledge that I'll soon have the camera, and everything will then be wrapped up permanently.

Looking around the living area, the most apparent difference from then to now is the removal of all the weapons and armour that were on wall display, replaced with watercolour paintings of castles and coastlines. Walking slowly through the room, I notice it has a less historic feel now, the calmer setting promoting a less militaristic environment. This is probably a wise change, given what the previous décor implements were used for.

Recalling there was a small set of hop-up steps in the utility room, I make my way there first and retrieve them, then head to the downstairs bedroom at the rear of the cottage. Opening the door slowly and seeing the bed and furniture as it was when I first walked into that room, I get a sudden rush back to that night, vividly seeing them both on the bed as I creep in with the sword, slowly raising it above my head. I feel the rage within me, giving me an almost superhuman strength that I focus on them. I feel the resistance pressure as I plunge the sword hard down into Craig's back, applying more and more pressure, intent on pushing it through him and into Tanya. I sense the slight movement changes in the sword handle as the blade is deflected by bone, finding a path of least resistance through softer tissue and organs. Craig arches his back, throwing his shoulders up, and I hear his scream of pain, then see the look of sheer horror on Tanya's face, trapped beneath him, as I proceed to pin them to the bed. That couple of seconds when Tanya saw me with the sword as I brought it down into Craig, and how she saw it was continuing to move downward through him, the realisation it was long enough to penetrate through him into her, watching her frantically trying to free herself of Craig's mass. The look on her face when the blade broke free of Craig's chest and continued its slide into hers, her eyes widening to the extent they looked like they would pop out of her skull. She has no scream, frozen in fear. As the blade cuts into her, she gags for a second, a reflex action of the blade driving into her chest; it twists ever so slightly as I apply more pressure to force steel through her ribs and into her heart. I have most of my body weight hanging on the sword hilt, driving it downward with a determination to push the sword's cross guard to meet Craig's back. Watching that last second of breath from Tanya was sheer ecstasy. The release I felt was like escaping from a trapped car beneath water and emerging at the surface, the oxygen intake smashing into me.

Looking at them both, Craig lying on top of Tanya, both impaled by the sword, I am surprised at how little blood there is. This is no slashing horror scene portrayed in the movies; this is a precision, almost surgical, use of a weapon designed for a specific function that it does so well. The white sheet over Craig's back is soaking up red blood from around the entry point, and the sheets beneath Tanya are red with blood, but this is gravity-draining blood, not spurts or splatter patterns. The bedding has helped contain the blood flow, and if it wasn't for the Sword hilt protruding from Craig's back, they could easily be covered with a duvet, and no one would know they've been killed so graphically.

The sound of a tractor in a nearby field brings me out of the trance I've entered. I'm still standing in the bedroom doorway, my breathing shallow and excited, and with my senses returning slowly, I'm looking at the empty bed, all made up for the next occupants, towels folded neatly at the foot. That was a rush; I didn't anticipate anything like that; yes, I knew what I'd done, but the finer details had been locked away deep in me. I had not appreciated that I had thoroughly enjoyed the act of killing them both in the way I did. I take a deep breath, exhale slowly, and remember why I'm here.

Placing the hop-up steps below the air vent, I climb the two steps and remove the screwdriver set from my jacket pocket. Removing the four corner screws carefully and placing them in my pocket, I pull the light aluminium grille away from the wall and see the little black camera lens looking at me. Reaching in, I remove the camera and place it in my inside pocket, returning the grille and replacing the four screws.

As I tighten the last screw, I wipe down the grille with my handkerchief to remove any trace of fingerprints; one can't be too careful. Backing down the two steps, as my left foot lands on the wooden floor, I sense a presence in the room; I start to turn to look over my shoulder, but the voice shudders me to a standstill.

'And what do you have there, Martin?'

49

DC Jo Hansen – Bramblehurst Police Station

It's my first time visiting this small backwater police station, and I'm surprised they are still in operation. The building must be at least one hundred years old, and by the looks of the two cell doors, they are original fittings. Only the door locks look modern—well, I say modern.

The local Inspector was already waiting for me to arrive, and I thanked him for his cooperation and the use of his officers and facilities. I suppose it's not often you get a big town detective coming to villages like this and it's linked to a double murder case, most likely the biggest crime that has happened in these parts since the police station was built.

Martin was directed straight to a cell when I saw that the interview room wasn't exactly a secure room on a secure floor. Now we've had a chance to tidy the room up a little, I've asked for him to be brought in for a formal interview, and when he enters the room, the young, uniformed constable is still setting up the laptop, a small camera on a tabletop tripod and a plug-in card reader.

Looking at Martin, he seems deflated. 'Come in, Martin, take a seat.'

'Am I under arrest, again?' his first words indicating he is already on the offensive.

'No, absolutely not. Apologies for placing you in a cell when you arrived; as you can tell from looking around, there is not much available space in here, and we needed to clear this room out before we could use it.

Please,' indicating to the old wooden chair opposite me, 'take a seat.'

He sits, and the constable boots up the laptop, 'Won't be a minute, er, Ma'am.'

'It's OK. There's no rush; let's make sure everything is working properly before we start.' He doesn't need to call me Ma'am, as technically we are both constables, but I quite like the sound of it and don't correct him. I look to Martin, 'Would you like a drink, Martin, a cup of tea, water?'

'No, thank you. Can we just get on with this, whatever this is?'

His frustration is evident. Is he worried about what may be on the nanny camera?

'OK, Ma'am, all good.'

'Thank you. Please stand by the door.'

'Er, yes, Ma'am.'

I make sure the video camera and audio are running to capture this interview.

'Now, Martin, first I will put you under caution, but I do stress this is a formality, and you are not being charged or are under arrest; you are helping us with our enquiries; is that clear?'

'Strange that, I've heard all this before.'

'Martin Nicholson, this interview will be conducted under caution. You do not have to say anything. But it may harm your defence if you do not mention when questioned something which you later rely on in court. Anything you do say may be given in evidence. Do you understand?'

'Yes, I do, only too well.'

'Please say your full name for the recording.'

He sighs, 'Martin Nicholson.'

'Present with Martin Nicholson is Detective Constable Joanna Hansen and PC…?' looking toward the young constable.

'Oh, er, PC Steven Winston.'

I nod, 'Thank you. We are at Bramblehurst Police Station, the date is Monday, the sixth of May, and the time is…,' looking at my wristwatch, 'fourteen forty-two.' I look directly at Martin and note he appears uncomfortable; he keeps looking away from me; he doesn't want to make eye contact and is fidgeting slightly. 'Martin, you contacted the owner of the holiday cottage called Fell View Cottage, which is located just outside Bramblehurst village, on Thursday of last week, asking for permission to return to the cottage. Is that correct?'

'Yes.'

I continue, 'Fell View Cottage was the scene of a double murder that took place on or about the evening or early hours of the tenth and eleventh of June last year. You were staying in the cottage at the time of the murders of your wife, Tanya Nicholson, and your friend, Craig Tyler; is that correct?'

'Yes, of course it is. It's a matter of fact.'

'You arranged to meet the cottage owner, a Mr… Rory Fraser, there earlier today.'

'Yes.'

'Please can you explain your reasons for returning to the cottage?'

'I don't see why my reasons are of interest to you, but I am curious to know why you are following me?'

'The police are not following you, Martin. After you called Mr Fraser to arrange the return to the cottage, he mentioned your conversation to his wife, and she commented that you had been in the news recently regarding another accidental death in another cottage in which you almost died. The Frasers checked on the internet and thought it was a little odd, and, as I had left my card with them last year, they called me as they were unsure if it was just a coincidence or possibly something else.'

'Umm.'

'You informed Mr Fraser that you wanted to return to the cottage as it may help with your recovery; it seems you are experiencing sleep and mood problems; is that correct?'

'Yes, wouldn't you, after what I've been through?'

'Probably.' His tone is curt, defensive almost. I know he's been through a lot, but I need to be sure he wasn't instrumental in what occurred. I continue, 'You met Mr Fraser at noon today at the cottage and within fifteen minutes of arriving there, you had retrieved some step ladders from the utility room, entered the downstairs bedroom, the scene of the murders, climbed up, unscrewed, and removed an air vent cover near the ceiling to recover an object. Would you mind telling me what the object is that you recovered?'

'I don't need to; it's in that plastic bag on the table in front of you.'

'For the interview recording, Martin is indicating the contents of a police evidence bag which contains a small portable covert camera, a video recording device. Is this your camera, Martin?'

'No.'

'Yet, you knew it was there and retrieved it. If it's not yours, who does it belong to, and how did you know it was there?'

'Look, I don't want to say, OK.'

'I'm sorry, Martin, if that is your answer, I would have to assume it is yours and you put it in the air vent, positioned to watch over the bed and record the murders.'

'No. No. That's not right,' shaking his index finger at me but looking down to his lap. 'It wasn't there for that.' His shoulders drop, and he exhales deeply.

'Well then, for what other reason could it be there?'

I wait for him to answer. He is thinking it through, and right now, it doesn't look good for him. I've caught him removing a vital piece of evidence, one that may have recorded the murders; he knew it was there, and yet he didn't say anything about it.

A minute or so passes, he raises his head and looks straight at me, 'It was Melissa's.'

'I'm sorry? You mean Melissa Tyler?'

'Yes.'

'But why didn't either of you say something about its existence at the time of the murders?'

'It's complicated.'

'I expect it is. Well, you had best explain it slowly, clearly and in full.'

He pauses for a few seconds, 'OK, I will. Melissa booked the cottage; she knew it had a third bedroom downstairs. She had known Tanya and Craig were having an affair; she planted the camera to film them so she could use it to leverage a decent divorce settlement. Craig was a lawyer, and she felt she needed some embarrassing evidence to support her cause.'

'OK, so running with that, was it Melissa that drugged the white wine?'

'Yes,' he said with deep sighs again. 'I know Melissa drugged the wine; she confirmed it at my Bothy.

She needed the two of us out of the way so they would go and use the third bedroom.'

I realise I am nodding slightly and stop immediately; I don't want him to think I'm affirming his story. 'So, this camera would have filmed Hatzis coming into the room and murdering them. So, why didn't Melissa mention this before?'

'She told me she was concerned because she had drugged the wine to set up the opportunity for the two of them to be together, but you would look to link her with Hatzis and accuse her of joint enterprise with him. She also said that if she hadn't drugged the wine, then maybe they wouldn't have been murdered. She was heavily plagued by this, torturing herself with guilt.'

'So how do you know she wasn't working with Hatzis?'

'She told me she wasn't, and I believed her.'

'When did she share this information with you?'

'The night we were in my Bothy, you found us the following day. We talked into the night, and I was comforting her.'

That explains it more clearly for me now; I know they weren't in bed together; they weren't sleeping like a couple.

'OK, so why did you return to the cottage earlier today to retrieve the camera?' On asking this, he drops his head again and looks at his lap. Slowly raising his head and looking back at me, he starts his reply, 'Because if you found it, you would have pieced a story together that wasn't true. I wanted Melissa to remain a victim in all this, especially after the accident at my Bothy. I wanted to protect her reputation and memory.'

'Really? Her reputation and memory? That's quite noble of you. Or could it be that there is something on this camera that you don't want to be seen?' His expression changes instantly; he looks nervous.

'I'm not sure what you mean?'

'Well, this camera model is designed for wireless use, pinging a video via the Wi-Fi within the cottage to a log-in cloud site; we will need to obtain a warrant to access the site to view the recording. However, we can possibly sidestep that hurdle now as it also has a small removable memory card inside it, as a backup in case the signal is lost.' I pull out a pair of blue sterile gloves and start pulling them on. 'Shall we see what's on it?'

50

Martin – Bramblehurst Police Station

'Shall we see what's on it?' she says confidently.

Damn it. I just knew something like this could happen; fucking technology. Watching her slowly pulling on some gloves, I can only hope that what Melissa said was true: that she had wiped the cloud video, and in doing so, it also wiped the memory card.

'Are you OK, Martin? You look a bit peaky.' Her question startles me out of my thoughts.

'Er, yes. Could I have a glass of water, please?'

She turns her head to the constable, 'Can you get a glass of water for Mr Nicholson, please?'

'Er, yes, Ma'am.'

I watch him as he opens the door, leaves, and closes it behind him. It's not a locking door; there is no pass card or PIN code, just a simple door handle. What do I do? Do I run for it? There is a good chance I can get out of here if I punch her hard, surprise her, or do I gamble that there is nothing on the video card? How confident was Melissa that she had wiped it? She seemed pretty satisfied that she had wiped it from the cloud but didn't know if it had an in-built memory card; now we know it does. This camera could really do for me now. My right leg is bouncing on my toes under the table. No, I can't wait to see if it recorded me; the constable will be back any second; if I'm doing this, it has to be now. She's fiddling with the camera, trying to remove the memory card, her head lowered over it. I can just smash her hard now, stun her.

There is a firm knock at the door, and it opens abruptly. The constable is standing there holding a plastic cup of water, and another copper, a senior officer, is standing beside him. My opportunity to run has just disappeared.

The senior officer standing just outside the door asks, 'Is everything OK, Detective Constable?'

'Yes, Sir,' she replies while still trying to remove the memory card. 'Aha, there we go, gotcha.' Holding the small card between thumb and index finger, she turns to look at the men in the doorway. 'Yes, everything is good, Sir. Thank you, constable.'

For a brief second, I thought of snatching it out of hand and swallowing it, but I don't know if that would destroy the content. I don't know. My leg is bouncing faster.

'OK, I'll leave it in your capable hands. I'll be right outside, just here, if you need anything.'

'Thank you, Sir; I'm in good hands; Constable Winston is doing a good job looking after us.'

I notice the constable smile slightly as he places the cup in front of me; verbal praise in front of his senior officer pleases him. The Inspector is keen to get involved but it's clear she doesn't want him interfering with her interview, pulling rank.

'Jolly good, I'm here if needed.'

'Thank you, Sir. Constable, could you please close the door so we can continue?'

'Yes, Ma'am.'

She turns her attention back to the memory card, 'Now, let's see what this camera has recorded, shall we?' She picks up the multi-card reader, pushing the small card into the appropriate slot. She turns the laptop so that we can both see the screen; slowly, she moves the cursor across the screen to the reader controls and clicks on the video file. The screen goes black for a second, and the white play arrow pops up in the middle of the display. 'OK, and… if we click here…'

I feel my teeth biting into my bottom lip and both my legs nervously moving up and down faster now. Just get on with it; I don't need the running commentary.

The screen image changes, and the third bedroom pops up, viewed through the horizontal bars of the air vent. I sink into my plastic chair, wishing the ground would open now and swallow me, the chair and everyone else in here. I should have run when I had the chance. I catch her flashing a brief glance at me and then back to the screen. I look to the door again; could I make it?

'Well, we do have video; who'd have thought it, after all this time.'

Winston, at the end of the table, is standing directly in my path to the door. I'll have to drop him first, then her and barge out, fighting whoever is on the other side.

'That's interesting,' she says quietly. She reaches out for the laptop and spins it back in front of herself. I see her move her middle finger on the laptop touchpad and tap keys frantically.

'What is?' I ask, but she doesn't reply. 'Detective?'

'Just a second, I need to check something.' She seems agitated and distracted. Is there something on that video she wasn't expecting?

I pick up my water and drink it all down in one, keeping a close watch on the constable by the door. He's leaning to his right, trying to see what the Detective is looking at and what she is doing. Then it occurs to me that she's obviously distracted by what she is seeing, so I try a move.

'Constable Winston, I could use a toilet break. Is it OK if I go now?'

He looks at me and then at the Detective, 'Ma'am, is it OK if I take Mr Nicholson to the toilet?'

She looks up briefly to him, then to me, 'Yes, but stay with him, please.'

I want to ask her why I need to be accompanied, seeing as I'm not under arrest or have been charged; using her own words, I'm merely assisting with enquiries, but I need her to stay distracted on the laptop and not give me a second thought. I stand, follow the constable out of the room, and I register the senior officer talking to a female constable across the small open-plan office. We turn right, and I follow the constable down a narrow corridor to a pale blue painted door with a "Gents" toilet sign above it. He steps to one side, and as I pass him, I quietly say, 'I'll be a couple of minutes.'

'No problem, Sir, I'll just wait here outside.'

That's what I wanted to hear. I enter the toilet and close the door behind me; only then do I realise it is nothing more than a cubicle room with a toilet and sink, and I lock the door behind me. Damn it; I thought it would be a bigger toilet room, and there would be a decent size window I could climb out of. The window in here is small, with an even smaller vent opener, there is no way I can climb up there and fit through it. I put the toilet seat and lid down and sit down, putting my head in my hands. I'm done for now. The camera was obviously working, and there is video on the memory card; Melissa thought she had wiped it clean but hadn't. As soon as Hansen gets to the recording capturing me killing them, I'll be arrested for sure. There is nothing to lose now; if I stay, I'm done; if I run, I might get away; I'll take the latter option over twenty to thirty years in prison any day. Melissa is not here now to say that her drugs may have caused me to sleepwalk or act in the way I did; her death, and now me not mentioning the camera and what Melissa said to me, would only look like I'm making it up as a feeble attempt at a defence of being not guilty of murder but maybe of manslaughter on the grounds of diminished responsibility. I look around this small toilet; there is nothing I can use as a weapon. The water cistern for the toilet is high and uncovered; there is no lid I can use to bludgeon anyone who tries to stop me.

Sitting, contemplating going berserk and attacking anyone who gets in my way, it's beginning to frighten me; my hands are shaking slightly, and I can feel frustration building in me. I had got away with this. That bloody camera: I should have just left it there.

The knocking at the door brings me to a focus. I stand, tensing my shoulders and arms, making fists, and taking deep breaths. I am psyching myself up for the fight. Then the next knock is followed by the constable's voice, 'Mr Nicholson, are you OK in there?'

It has to be now. I reach for the sliding lock on the door, and as my fingers take hold of the handle, I hear another voice outside the door, a deeper voice, one I've not heard before.

'Is everything OK there, Stevie lad?'

'Aye, Sarge, just waiting for Mr Nicholson to come out.'

No, I can't do this; there are at least four people out there now, not counting Hansen, and I have no chance of overpowering all of them. I will have to play the diminished responsibility line and hope it works. I lift and slide the bolt back and open the door. Instantly, it is clear I made the right choice; the Sergeant is built like a Marine, at least six inches taller than me, broad and very fit-looking. Our eyes meet briefly, and he comments in his booming voice, 'Good afternoon, Sir.' My reply acknowledges his comment, and I walk into the corridor to head back to the small interview room. As I walk slowly, over and over in my head, I repeat to myself, "*Stay calm, use your wits. Stay calm, win the day. Stay calm; you need to act surprised; you don't recall any of this; this is a shock.*"

Entering the room, I take the same seat I vacated a few minutes ago, and Constable Winston stands by the door again. I look at Hansen and she doesn't show any emotion or demonstrate any portrayal of her being the victor. I take the opportunity to speak first.

'Detective. I recognised the bedroom from that video recording. What else has it captured?'

'Well, the camera was working until its battery ran out.'

'So, it captured Hatzis killing them then?'

'It seems the camera is activated on motion detection, so it is intermittent, there are hours or days between recordings.'

'And?'

'And… well… it seems that it only started recording about four or five days after the incident.'

'Really? Are you sure?' this is a lucky break for me.

'Yes. The earliest recording is of a couple of the forensic team returning to the room to carry out further testing; then, it jumps to a couple of guys sealing the mattress in plastic sheeting and removing it. Next, it shows a clean-up team scrubbing the room clean about two weeks after the murders, then nothing for about four or five weeks, when housekeeping returns with a new mattress and bedding and the room is made up for new guests. Each recording has a date and time stamp. There is nothing before the fifteenth of June.'

I can't believe what I'm hearing. She only went and did it! Melissa scrubbed the cloud recording, which must have cleared the recording on the memory card at the same time. There is no recording of me in the room. Thank you, Melissa. I want to cheer but must remain composed like I never expected anything to be found that would incriminate me.

'So, Detective, we nearly had the video of Hatzis killing them, but it now seems we haven't.'

'Yes, well, I'll get the tech guys to look at this a little closer and see what they can do with it.'

'Why?' This seems like a sensible question if I'm not a suspect.

'Well, er, it would, er, be good to have something that would confirm Hatzis did this.'

'What, you still don't accept that he did it?' She doesn't reply. She takes the memory card out of the card reader, puts it back in the nanny cam and then places both back in the evidence bag.

'So, if there is nothing else, Detective, am I free to go now?'

'Erm… yes, Martin, there is nothing further you can assist us with. It appears you are either a very lucky man, Martin, or unlucky in that you seem to be in the wrong places at the wrong time.'

'As I mentioned before, I think I'm unlucky when all things are considered, wouldn't you agree?'

'Yes, I suppose so. However, I will have to report your reluctance to come forward with information about this hidden camera and your attempt to recover it today.'

'Well, you must do what you think is right, Detective, although I'm not sure my solicitor will take kindly to you trying to pursue some further allegation against me when I have done nothing to hinder or hamper your investigation. I am the victim here; that seems to be overlooked by the police. I've lost my wife and a friend to murder, and… no, in fact, I've lost my wife and two friends to murder, and narrowly avoided becoming a fourth murder victim myself. We had this issue before when your colleagues charged me with murder, only to find out someone else had done it. I think I will be the one discussing this further with my solicitor and the police complaints authority. Now, I'm leaving, and no doubt, you will be hearing from my solicitor in due course; please keep the recording of this interview as I will be requesting a copy.'

As I finish speaking, I realise I should have toned that right back; that would have come across as cocky and arrogant; it was probably the adrenalin still coursing through me and the relief that I very nearly ruined it all by running away. But then again, I am the aggrieved party here, being pursued by the police, so I should be rightly upset. Standing, I push the chair backwards with my legs, and the back of the chair hits the wall with a clatter. 'Good afternoon, Detective.'

Out on the street in front of the Police Station, I realise my car is still at the cottage. It's three thirty-five, and I recall Rory saying he had advised the next occupants they couldn't enter until after four o'clock. There is just enough time to return to my car and drive away before they arrive. Picking up the pace, I stride out towards the cottage, taking the route we all took the afternoon, crossing fields and through the woods to the cottage.

51

Martin – Home, Northampton

Sunday Morning, 26th May

It's a lovely early summer sunny Sunday morning and having bought a selection of Sunday newspapers from my local newsagent, I slowly wander back home, wearing sunglasses and my wireless headset, listening to a true crime podcast. It always amazes me how some criminals get caught by doing the most stupid of things or not thinking about the small details that will trip them up. Engrossed in the discussion, I didn't notice the dark windowed car slowly crawling up alongside me and pulling up just ahead, but I did see the front passenger door open and a large, thickset, but well-dressed guy step out in front of me and block my path.

We look at each other, not two feet apart. His lips are moving, but I can't hear him, and realise I have my headset on, drowning him out. Pulling the headset backwards, I let it fall and rest around the back of my neck and on my shoulders, then look up at him.

'Sorry, I missed that; you were saying?'

He speaks again. 'Mr Nicholson. Come with us, please,' and he opens the rear passenger door, clearly intending that I should get in.

'Er, whoa, sorry, and you are?'

He gestures to the open car door, 'It will be in your interest to come along, Sir.'

'I think not, thank you. I don't know who the hell you are!'

From within the car, an accented voice calls out, 'For God's sake, Martin, just get in the car.'

I look at the guy standing in front of me, 'And if I don't want to?'

'You'll find you do. Inside... *please*,' he says with an indication of menace if I don't comply.

'Well, how can I refuse such a polite invitation; it looks like we're going for a drive.'

I pass my newspapers to the guy, who takes them without comment. Placing my hand on the car's roof, I lower myself to look inside and see a familiar face, but one I can't quite place at the moment. 'Hello, and where are we going?'

He replies as I climb into the back seat, 'Hello Martin, we're off for a little drive. My Boss would like to speak with you,' and no sooner do I pull my legs into the car than the guy outside closes the door behind me. 'He wants to have a quiet chat with you; I presume you have time this morning for a chat?'

'Er, yes, no problem.' I'm not sure who these guys are, but they're certainly not the police.

Thickset guy gets into the front passenger seat, and I feel the car settle further under his mass. The driver indicates, looks over his shoulder, and pulls away from the kerb. My backseat companion hands me a black cotton bag, 'Put that on.'

Another instruction I presume not to refuse, so I pull the bag over my head. It is not completely dark, and I can make out images, although heavily obscured.

As we pick up speed, I hear the doors auto-locking, or did the driver do that on purpose? I can feel my phone in my trouser pocket, tight against my thigh, but I'll struggle to get it free without him noticing, sitting beside me in the back. I turn to my fellow passenger, 'So, what is this about?'

'You'll know soon enough; my Boss prefers to do things face to face, you know, all personal like.'

'And your Boss is?'

'You'll find out soon enough. I'll take your mobile phone, please?' and I feel him tap the phone pinned against my leg.

I squirm and fish it out of my pocket, and a few seconds later, I hear the tell-tale 'off' blip.

There is no more conversation during the next half hour or so as we drive out of town, heading towards East Brampton. If these men represent the person that I think I'm going to meet, then I know he won't want to meet me in a public place, so I expect I'm being taken somewhere very private. If it's not who I think it is, then I could be in a lot of trouble here. I should have asked some more questions before I got in this car; I should have turned around and walked away.

I can make out the wider roads have reduced to country lanes now, and we are slowing due to the narrow widths and tight bends, with hedges and overhanging tree cover. He speaks again, 'OK, you can take the hood off now.'

I pull it off and place it on the seat space between us. As I run my fingers across my scalp, trying to tidy up my hair, I try some dialogue: 'This looks interesting; it's a bit remote though,' I quip, then instantly regret it; it is quite remote.

'Yes, it's a little off the beaten track, just the way he likes it.'

The road opens a little wider now and straightens, with a six-foot high brick and stone wall running alongside the road on our right, the kind of wall you'd expect to see around an old country estate. The car slows as it approaches an entrance to a property, swinging in onto a gravel road. Large, solid-looking wooden gates open slowly as we approach them, and we continue through without coming to a stop. Looking around, I notice at least three CCTV cameras, one on each of the brick gate pillars and another just inside the gate at low level, looking directly into the car at driver level; this is obviously a property where the occupier has a penchant for feeling secure; this is reinforced when I see two guards patrolling with leashed guard dogs and shotguns, broken, slung over their forearms like they are wandering off to a pheasant shoot.

The car continues along the gravel road, crunching its way down towards a large Elizabethan manor house set in rolling green fields with the obligatory private lake in the distance. We sweep past the main house and manicured lawns and continue down one side, slowing to a crawl, entering a large courtyard area bounded on three sides with stables and a coach house. The driver turns the car in a large circular sweep to point it towards an arch doorway in one of the buildings, entering the old coach house before bringing the vehicle to a stop.

Short of something to say, I can only muster, 'Impressive.'

'Yes, it is, isn't it.'

The car doors unlock with a gentle uniform click, and my three companions open their doors and step out. I suppose I'm expected to do the same.

'If you don't mind, Martin, this way.' My rear seat companion heads off through the coach house, and I follow him, with my new front seat passenger friend bringing up the rear. We walk through a stables block, on cobbled floors covered here and there with strewn straw, horses clattering quietly in stables. Breaking out of the building into bright sunlight, we continue along a paved path heading towards the rear of the manor house. I see two more dog walkers, complete with shotguns, patrolling the rear gardens.

'You get the odd trespasser around here, do you?' I project forward, a feeble attempt at some levity.

He looks back over his shoulder, 'Haha, not often, but when we do, they don't tend to return.'

'Um, I can see why.'

Following him up a small flight of stone steps, we walk across a lawn to a large patio area dotted with several pruned bushes in large planting urns. We head toward three umbrella-covered tables, each with wooden chairs and cushions, and two sun loungers off to one side.

Back seat guy lays out his left hand, indicating I should take a seat at one of the tables. 'Boss will be here shortly. Please make yourself comfortable. Some refreshments will be brought out to you.'

'Thank you,' and I take a seat, looking out over the landscaped gardens towards the lake at the bottom. Both men turn to walk away, although they don't go far, maybe only twenty metres or so, before they both turn back towards me and stand with their hands crossed in front of them at waist level. It is beginning to feel like I'm amid a small, private army.

It is peaceful, though, the odd swallow, swooping and dancing the gentle breeze. I close my eyes, tipping my head back slightly and taking in the sun and gentle birdsong. Within a few minutes, the sound of a distant vehicle cuts into the tranquillity, getting louder and closer. I open my eyes, tip my head forward, and see two four-wheel drive vehicles rounding a distant wood by the lake, driving a track along the edge of the field, kicking up small dust trails. The two black Range Rovers swing out wide, and I lose sight of them behind the stable block and coach house. Everything goes quiet, and birdsong returns, tranquillity restored.

Then I see him exit the stable block, followed closely by two aides, for want of a better expression. All three of them are dressed in country gentleman attire: the obligatory tweed waistcoats and what look like matching Derby tweed flat caps. I smile to myself, ever so slightly shaking my head from side to side.

He bounds up the steps, two at a time and swiftly crosses the lawn and patio, his arms outstretched; I stand to greet him with slight relief, knowing I am safe, and he bellows out first in a confident and calm tone, 'Hello, Martin, why has it been so long?'

'Hello, Nico.'

He grabs me in a bear hug, lifts me from the floor, and kisses me on both cheeks before planting me back down on terra firma. He steps back with his hands on his hips, 'You are looking well, Martin, maybe a little thin, I'm thinking,' and he laughs out loud.

'Whereas you look nothing like the landed gentry that used to own this place,' I reply.

He laughs again, 'Only you could say that to me and still be standing there.' He steps forward, grabbing a chunk of my left cheek between his thumb and forefinger and pulling at it, 'You always were the cheeky little runt. Come here,' and he hugs me again.

Letting me go after almost squeezing the marrow out of my bones, he turns toward the table and says, 'Come sit.' He pulls back a chair and calls out, 'Tony, get us some champagne to celebrate.'

Back seat passenger snaps to and replies, 'Yes, of course, Mr Costas.'

52

Martin – Arberly Manor, Northamptonshire

It's been a long time since I've seen Nico. He looks well, and obviously, the Developer business is lucrative; well, the lucrative Developer front needed to launder cash from all his other business ventures. The level of security around him has surprised me though.

Tony returns carrying a silver ice bucket containing a bottle of champagne, followed closely by a maid with a silver tray holding glasses and a large bowl of strawberries partly coated in chocolate; they place them on the table.

'Thank you,' Nico says generally, 'Please, we require some privacy; leave us,' which is taken by all present who depart without comment. Nico pours champagne into two glasses and picks up the bowl, offering me a strawberry.

'No, thank you, I don't snack between meals.'

'Haha, this is why you are so thin. Come, take one, you'll enjoy it,' he replies, thrusting the bowl in front of me.

'OK, if it pleases you.'

He hands me a glass and holds his out by the narrow stem to me, 'To Nico and Martin, stin ygeiá mas!'

I reply, 'Stin ygeiá mas,' and we each take a long drink of champagne. As I place my glass on the table, there is no better time to ask him, 'Why have you brought me here, to your home?'

'No, please, do not presume, this is not my home; it belongs to my second wife from her first marriage, a very expensive weekend retreat which she enjoys.'

'Ah, you have married again?'

'Yes, one changes one's mind every now and again,' he chuckles. 'Yes, I invited you here as I wanted to clear the air between us to be sure there is no, how shall I put it, misunderstanding.'

'I'm not sure what you mean, Nico.'

He takes another strawberry and bites it in two, slowly enjoying the morsel, before he replies. 'Hatzis. That was all rather unfortunate, no?'

I did wonder whether it was Nico who sent him that weekend. Now, I get to ask and find out what happened. 'Yes, unfortunate, but his suicide in prison had nothing to do with me. I don't have that kind of reach.'

'No, that was my doing; it was a necessity; that is not the misunderstanding that concerns me. Because that lawyer mongrel, Tyler, would not play ball with my insurance settlement, I wanted to acquire some, shall I say, leverage to help persuade him. I was informed he was having an affair with another man's wife and that they would be in the cottage that weekend. Hatzis was to enter the cottage and photograph them in flagrante delicto, Tyler would call it, caught red-handed with his mistress. His reputation and image were important to him, as were his money and property. He would do almost anything to avoid a very public divorce and humiliation.'

'Yes, he was very conscious about his image. But unfortunately, Nico, his mistress, was my wife.'

'Umm, so it seems. I was not aware of that; this is the misunderstanding that concerns me.

'How so? Hatzis is dead, and the police have closed the matter now.'

'Well, Hatzis did not kill them. I know this, as he would not lie to me or disobey a clear instruction.' He refills his glass and leans towards me to fill mine and stops, the bottle poised in mid-pour, 'They were killed in a most curious way, one that exudes a certain passion, a certain flair. One that I recognised.'

'Look, I am sorry about your man, Hatzis; it was all unfortunate timing.'

'No, do not misunderstand me; I do not mourn Hatzis; in fact, I celebrate his timely sacrifice. The necessity of his suicide looked to all concerned that it was for my self-preservation, and I can live with that, when in fact, it was totally to do with protecting you, my baby brother.'

It's been a long time since he referred to me as his baby brother, and it feels good to be a part of something again.

'But how did you know it was me that killed them?'

'At first, I did think it was Hatzis, that something must have gone wrong, but then the news indicated that the victim's friend and her husband, Martin Nicholson, was helping the police with their enquiries. I thought maybe the name was a coincidence, but then I saw a photo of you leaving the police station, and well, I knew something had to be done to protect you, just like you protected me all those years ago.'

All those years ago, another lifetime, a different lifetime. He continues.

'But Martin, I could not help you directly; if the police connected us, we would both have been arrested. So, Hatzis had to be killed by suicide.' He shrugs his shoulders, 'Huh, the man wasn't that useful anyway.'

'Well, it worked. You saved the day, big brother. We are all square now.'

Nico raises his glass high in toast, 'To us, blood is blood.'

I clink his glass with mine, 'blood is blood.'

We drink quietly, looking at each other, both slowly and ever so gently nodding to each other. 'Blood is blood,' I repeat quietly.

'So, tell me, baby brother, why did you kill them? It seems like you did not plan it very well. It was lucky Hatzis turned up when he did.'

'Yes, Hatzis and Melissa.'

'Melissa?'

'Melissa Tyler, Craig's wife, planned to photograph them as well, that is, video record them. She planted a nanny cam in the third bedroom, drugged my wine and hers so that we would sleep, expecting Craig and Tanya to carry on exactly the way they did downstairs.'

'This camera and video; where is this now?'

'It's with the police.' This startles him, 'No, don't worry, the video has been erased from the camera; it's useless. Just as well, as it would have filmed me killing them.'

'So, if this Melissa drugged you, how did you kill them before Hatzis got there?'

'Well, at the beginning of last year, I was in a bit of a bad way; my latest book bombed, and I wasn't the hit anymore. I went to see a private doctor, as I didn't want my illness out in the public domain, and he prescribed some sedatives, sleeping pills, which at first worked but then became less effective as the weeks passed. He kept upping the dose, but after another few weeks of increasing the dose, the doctor said I have a rare condition, tachyphylaxis.'

'Oh, no, this is not serious, is it, Martin?' He reaches across the gap between us and places his large right hand on the back of my left hand. His concern is genuine.

'No, no, it's OK, it's nothing to worry about. It just means I become tolerant to certain drugs over time, such that I need to increase the dosage to get the same effect. The dosage Melissa gave me was enough for me to fall asleep, but just for a couple of hours. I woke thirsty, went downstairs for a glass of water, and heard them in the third bedroom.

'So, what happened?'

He is quietly sitting and looking at me, still with his hand on the back of mine. I take a large swallow of champagne, and he lets go of my hand to refill my glass. 'I woke up just after two in the morning, and Tanya was not beside me. I went downstairs for a glass of water, and I heard a couple at it in the spare bedroom. Knowing Melissa went to bed after what I thought was too much wine, it could only have been Craig and Tanya. I slowly opened the door, enough to peep in, and confirmed my suspicions. I was so full of anger at being betrayed by them both. Knowing that swords were readily available on the wall, I took one down and… killed them both. They deserved it. Only I know I did it and was compos mentis whilst doing it, channelling my anger to the pair of them for betraying me and my trust.

'Breaking that trust between two people is a terrible thing; it is not something that can be repaired.'

'To be honest, Nico, I never thought I'd get away with it. After I plunged the sword through them, I went back into the kitchen area, gulped down the last half bottle of white wine, and went back to bed, resigned to my fate in the morning. But, unbeknown to me at the time, that top-up of spiked wine re-dosed me enough to sleep through until the police were banging on the door a few hours later and the drug showed up in my blood samples.

'So, why was this Melissa of help to you?'

'She had the video of me killing them but thought I was sleepwalking, under the influence of the drugs, mixed with alcohol, that she had dosed me with. She felt compromised, that she had caused all this to happen.'

'So, she did know you had killed them?'

'Yes, but to protect herself and me, she wiped the video clean. She was the one who trusted in me.' I look at him, listening intently, empathising with his brother's dilemma. 'That night brought back all those feelings of that time with Papa.'

He closes his eyes and nods gently, 'Yes, I can see the similarities. Papa was a hard man.'

'He was worse after Mama jumped in front of that train; she abandoned us, left us with him.'

'Don't blame Mama, Martin; to her, that was the only way out back then.'

'But still...'

'If you hadn't stuck that kitchen knife in him that day, he would have killed me, you know that. You know you did the right thing. You saved me.'

This is the first time I've talked about this since all those therapy sessions in care. I feel anxious, burdened, like I'm being pushed down to the bowels of the earth again, fighting my demons once more. He doesn't say anything for a good few minutes; he just holds both my hands whilst I look down and close my eyes, fighting back tears.

Those days were incredibly horrible, tormented by what I'd done, the talking sessions with specialists, and the re-conditioning process they put me through. I know it all came good in the end when the Nicholsons, knowing my situation, adopted me and took me as their own; they gave me a good life and a happy childhood, with school and holidays far from my past life; the court sealed my files to give me a chance at a normal life; whatever one of those is.

Nico broke the silence, 'You were only five years old, Martin; it was tough on you. I lost my baby brother that day when he became a man before his time. When we were adopted by different families, we lost each other, and you were so young. But look, after we found each other again, you should have asked for my help; you can always rely on me, little brother.'

Shaking my head at him, 'No, I could not risk the police putting the two of us together. Ironically, I was going to contact you after that weekend; Craig told me it was someone from the Costas Group that had threatened him, and he had reported this to the police. I wanted to warn you, but when I saw him with Tanya that night, I knew I had to protect us both again, the only way I knew how to. However, now the police have my DNA on file, this could put you at risk.'

'Do not worry about our DNA; I have someone inside the police who can remove it. You are the God Ares, and I am Hades; we should stay together now, work together, be a family again.'

'No,' slowly shaking my head from side to side. 'No, brother; you have your world of various interests, and I have my world of writing. We have very different lives that would not go well together.'

'Do we? Do we really? It seems to me we still have much in common.'

53

DC Joanna Hansen – Mylesham Police Station

Monday, 27th May

I was happy in this station with this crowd, but someone higher has apparently seen some potential in me. The move to the regional crime team is an opportunity not to miss, although they've not given me much notice, told me yesterday and move out tomorrow. So, I have the rest of today set aside to clear my administration backlog, file, and hand over the two cases I'm currently working on to colleagues. This kind of opportunity doesn't come around often, and DI Robbins suggested I grab it and run with it, take it as far as it will go.

Sifting through the documents and folders in the wire basket on my desk, I'm coming across bits of information from various cases that I need to file correctly or shred if they are of no further use. I turn up my notes folder for the first case I was involved with months ago, the double murder of Nicholson and Tyler in the holiday cottage, and I open it, more for curiosity or nostalgia, and I sit back with a cup of tea and scan over my handwritten notes. Within the folder, there is the original transcript of my interview with Martin Nicholson at Bramblehurst Police Station, the surviving husband, after he went back to the cottage to retrieve that camera; this document should have been returned to the case file for scanning/digitising. I also have a paper print of the DNA results for Martin Nicholson, but I can't remember why I printed it out. I could have gotten into trouble for these procedural slips if things had turned out differently; I never really understood why it wasn't in the public interest to pursue Martin for not mentioning that camera, but that's the chiefs for you, one eye on their careers and the other on budgets.

Ah yes, this is the case that the offender, Hatzis, died in prison. Yes, it's coming back to me now, a poor attempt to make his demise look like a suicide or a good attempt at showing what treatment a police informant would receive; it's all about perspective, I suppose; either way, case closed.

Martin Nicholson; umm, he must be the luckiest unlucky person I've ever met.

I know I shouldn't do this, but I fold the original statement and the DNA report and put them in my laptop bag. The case files are all archived; to have the statement inserted now, I'll need to action someone to scan and file it, which could raise some awkward questions, and I don't want to be in any bad books before I get to my new station and new team. Anyway, the case is closed now; I can't see much harm in me doing this.

I'm looking forward to a new start tomorrow and my first investigation: organised crime.

54

Martin – Epilogue

Tuesday, 24th September

This is the first time I have flown first class on any airline. Leaving Heathrow behind me felt like an escape, off to a new venture and a new life in the US. The hostess smiles sweetly as she refills my glass as I push the button to recline my chair, stretching my legs to the footrest in front of the TV screen.

Looking out as we cut through clouds, climbing to cruising altitude, I'm impressed with myself. I committed two cold-blooded murders with a single sword stroke and got away with it. It was nearly three murders that night; to think, I went into Melissa's bedroom in the cottage and was about to suffocate her while she slept to spare her the misery and suffering of what was to come after I'd killed her husband and my wife; but, hovering over her, looking at her peacefully sleeping, I couldn't do it; she was an innocent. Although now I know she wasn't truly innocent that night, and yes, it was a lucky decision not to kill her. Maybe I am a lucky man?

It was good seeing Nico again, although we both accept the necessity of staying detached from one another; our lives are so diverse and successful in their different ways.

Actually, no; thinking about it, counting Papa, it is three that I've killed, although technically that was manslaughter; so, it still doesn't make me a serial killer, not just yet anyhow. *Is it also three murders in the US to be classed a serial killer?*

Landing that significant advance for my autobiography was welcome; adding to the life insurance and the income from the house and Bothy sales has made me quite a wealthy man with no ties. I have that meeting arranged in Los Angeles tomorrow to discuss film rights and options; it'll be interesting as I've decided to hold out for a say in the casting. I wonder who they are shortlisting to play me? Oh, and there are the talk shows in LA, Chicago, and New York to prepare for; busy times ahead.

I suppose I'll need to decide where to call my new home, the East Coast, or the West, or maybe even the Caribbean; there are one or two nice tax havens down there I should look into.

Crime doesn't pay, apparently.

Melissa and I, *could we have made it together?* I'd like to think so, but if I'm honest with myself, probably not. We each had too much personal baggage that would weigh us down, reminding us of it each time we met. It would also have been a lot to trust another person with my deepest secrets. At least her death is not on my conscience; that one is on her partner and her friend.

ALSO BY MARK HURST

The Lies

When Samantha and David decide to have a night out separately with their friends, events overtake them, and the lies lead them down a path of destruction.

To everyone else, it looked like Samantha and David had the perfect life. From meeting at university and falling in love to starting a successful business together, they made a great team. However, as everybody knows, appearances can be deceptive…

That one night out changed everything between them and things would never be the same again; not unless they could face up to their own truths and correct the wrongs.

Neither thought they could become the people they became and do the things they did. But that's just what happens when two people wronged become consumed by a need for the truth, for justice, and ultimately, for the price to be paid.

If either of them had let it go, it could have all been so different – but neither of them could.

The fast paced and gripping debut novel that will keep you turning the pages as you try to answer the question yourself – would you have let it go?

Lies Never Die

In the sequel to 'The Lies', Samantha and Blade continue playing the game of truth versus lie, reality against perception.

Dame Samantha Walsh, now a world icon, a person of respect, wealth and charity, flawless and untouchable in equal measure, continues to grow her empire on her terms. Her enormous wealth and reach bring about power and control never before contemplated, opening up new interests and outcomes for her, both inside and outside legal and moral boundaries.

Blade, recently released from prison, needing to re-integrate with society, has his path to follow to find the truth. He needs work, he needs income, and what better way to fund finding the truth than by taking paid work doing what he is good at, what he was trained to do?

The race is on to find out the truth of what happened to their loved ones. Who will find out first, who will win?

Fast paced and gripping, 'Lies Never Die' is the sequel to the bestselling debut book 'The Lies' from crime and psychological thriller author Mark Hurst.

A note from the author

Thank you for reading my book, I hope you found it entertaining. If you would like to pass a comment to me, please do so via email to mark@markhurstauthor.com and I will reply.

You may have already downloaded my FREE shorter story "The Last Woman", but if not, it is still available, please visit my web site at www.woodedhillbooks.com and click on the download link.

About the author

Born and raised in Bolton, UK, a true Lancastrian and a child of the sixties, Mark finally decided to pursue his passion for storytelling after a long and eventful career in a completely different industry, that sometimes involved more fiction than fact!

Mark entered construction at the age of eighteen and has been involved with hundreds of large civil engineering projects for the last 40 years as a Civil Engineer and Surveyor, Estimator and Commercial Director, working in various far-flung locations such as Hong Kong, Scandinavia and Wigan.

Mark has a passion for reading legal, crime and psychological thrillers and enjoys firsthand accounts of military and espionage events. When he's not reading and writing, he can be found watching the History Channel.

Married with two grown children and four grandchildren, his son Daniel convinced him it was time to start committing some of his own stories to print ... and there are a few. Drawing on his own life experiences, Mark weaves them into his stories but with a twist ... it all could have happened.

Why Wooded Hill Books?

The origin of the surname Hurst – ancient Anglo-Saxon topographic name for someone who lived near a wooded hill or thicket.

PLEASE KEEP IN TOUCH

Facebook.com/markhurstauthor

www.woodedhillbooks.com

Front cover design by 100Covers

Wooded Hill Books Limited

Printed in Great Britain
by Amazon

41345274R00158